'Thanks for

'Sure,' he said in a ... ...
he faced her.

He caught her eyes .... and looked so intently
into them that it crossed her mind that he was
searching for something. But she didn't know what.
Unless it was for a sign of the effect he'd had on her
by just holding her hand.

And he was still holding it. Caressing it now with light
strokes of his thumb that set off glittering sparks from
that spot all the way up her arm.

Then he kissed her.

She didn't see it coming. But she was so lost in what
his touch could do to her that even if there had been
signs of it, she knew she would have missed them.
She almost missed the kiss itself because it was so
quick, so brief. Really just a scant brushing of his lips
against hers.

Yet it was enough to go straight to her head. To make
her lean slightly forward, as if he might do it again.
Wishing he would…

He didn't, though. Instead he let her go, whispered
a soft, 'Night,' and left as if someone were chasing
him away.

And as she watched him go, she warned herself again
that she was on dangerous territory with him. The
man had power. Over her, at least. Power that made
her forget herself. Power that made it easy to forget
he was one of the richest men in the world.

world's most
Eligible Bachelors

VICTORIA PADE
Wyoming Wrangler

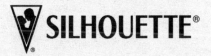

All the characters in this book have no existence outside the imagination of the author, and have no relation whatsoever to anyone bearing the same name or names. They are not even distantly inspired by any individual known or unknown to the author, and all the incidents are pure invention.

Silhouette and Colophon are registered trademarks of Harlequin Books S.A., used under licence.

First published in Great Britain 2003
Silhouette Books, Eton House, 18-24 Paradise Road,
Richmond, Surrey TW9 1SR

© Victoria Pade 1998

ISBN 0 373 65026 4

143-0403 DM

Printed and bound in Spain
by Litografia Rosés S.A., Barcelona

VICTORIA PADE

is the bestselling author of numerous contemporary romances, six historical romances and two mystery novels. She began her writing career after leaving college to have her first daughter. It was only after her daughter was seven years old, and she'd had her second daughter, that Victoria had her first book accepted for publication. That novel and the three that followed it were historical romances. But the exit of her husband and the urge to do more contemporary writing that explored the kinds of problems she was facing inspired a switch. Contemporary romances are still where her main interest lies, although she's enjoyed veering off the path into two more historical romances, as well as into mystery writing.

Victoria lives in Colorado where she shares a home with her parents, her younger daughter (who is a computer whiz), a college student studying psychology and Lucy the Schnauzer—resident prima donna and boss of the house. Her eldest daughter is now in Michigan attending medical school.

One

He's long. He's lean. But he ain't mean. And according to *Prominence Magazine,* Shane McDermot is one of the world's most eligible bachelors.

A maverick master of animal husbandry and the darling of this year's big event in Denver—the Stock Show—Shane raises an expansive, award-winning herd of cattle that yields the best beef this country and a number of other countries around the globe have tasted in a quarter of a century.

Beginning with only one bull that Shane brought with him from a trip to Europe, this cowboy has managed to make himself a multi-millionaire and one of America's richest ranchers. Not only is his succulent prime beef in high demand by meat markets, grocery chains and restaurants on nearly every continent, but it comes from animals so hardy they thrive in almost any environment, withstanding low temperatures and producing calves that can survive a winter birth—all factors that other ranchers are eager to introduce into their own herds.

Well, after meeting up with this cowpoke in

Cheyenne for a Cattleman's Association convention, we're here to tell you that *Prominence Magazine* knows whereof it speaks when it pinpoints this guy as someone worthy of tracking down and trying to lasso up good and tight. Because it isn't only the meat that comes from his Wyoming ranch that's luscious and succulent. The man himself is every bit as choice. He's bright, intelligent, funny, chivalrous, suave, sexy and more prime than any beef on the hoof.

He admits that he works more than he plays, but he definitely enjoys the company of women when that playtime comes around. So if you like your men the way you like your meat, and wouldn't mind giving up fast food and shopping malls to make a home on the range with this gorgeous hunk of bachelor, head your horse for a little town called Elk Creek, right here in Wyoming.

But be careful if you do, girls, because our man Shane says life has taught him to take business seriously and romance with a grain of salt.

Still, who knows? Any one of us could be just the woman to rein in this cowboy.

"Ma'am, I'd be much obliged if you'd put your shirt back on."

"Excuse me?" Maya Wilson said as she glanced up from the article she'd just read, letting her voice ring with every bit of her outraged disbelief that a stranger on a train would say such a thing to her.

The man was sitting in the seat facing hers, and in the hour since the train had departed from Cheyenne, she had barely glanced at him. Let alone taken off her shirt. Instead she'd been reading magazines like the *Cheyenne Monthly* with the silly piece about a man from Elk Creek, Wyoming. A man whose name she'd heard before but whom she'd never really met, even though Elk Creek was the small town in which she'd grown up. The small town where she was headed at that very moment. The small town she hadn't been back to more than a dozen times in the eleven years since she'd left.

Her seatmate grinned and—unless she was mistaken—had some trouble not laughing at her. He managed to contain his amusement and nodded upward, above her head, relaying a silent suggestion to look at something.

Maya pivoted enough to discover that standing behind her seat was a woman. But not just any run-of-the-mill woman. A beautiful woman who also happened to have the front of her T-shirt pulled up to expose extremely large, undeniably bare breasts.

"Oh my gosh!" Maya breathed in full shock at what she was seeing.

But the other woman wasn't paying attention to Maya. The other woman only had eyes for Maya's seatmate.

"These could all be yours," she said to the man in an exaggerated bedroom voice, lowering her eyelids to half-mast and running her tongue over her lips.

"Thanks very much, but no thanks," the man answered with as much western courtesy and aplomb as if she'd just offered him a sandwich when he wasn't the least hungry. "Now, how 'bout sittin' down? Please."

The woman let her eyes close the rest of the way and gave a sensual air kiss. But she finally pulled her shirt over her breasts and disappeared behind Maya's seat.

Still not quite believing what she'd seen, Maya would rather have had a root canal than turn and face the man across from her after what they'd both just witnessed—and after having made a fool of herself by thinking he'd been talking to her.

But she didn't have a choice.

So, wishing the heat she could feel in her cheeks didn't mean she was blushing, she slowly swiveled back around, averting her eyes rather than looking squarely at him.

But when her glance fell to the magazine in her lap—most particularly to the picture that accompanied the article she'd just read—her discomposure turned to something else.

She stared at the photograph, then raised her gaze to her seatmate to make sure she wasn't imagining things.

She wasn't.

Shane McDermot, the subject of the article, one of the world's most eligible bachelors, the darling of Denver's Stock Show, the multimillionaire cattleman and, coincidentally, the person she was headed to Elk Creek to take a closer look at, was the man sitting not two feet in front of her.

"Sorry about that," he said with a nod indicating where the woman had been.

But Maya barely heard him as her brain worked to reconcile who he was. She took a much, much closer look at him, registering for the first time just what she was looking at.

And what she was looking at was an awesomely attractive man.

He had hair that was a symphony of colors from pale brown to golden blond shot through with streaks so sun-kissed they were almost white. He wore it short. Very short on the sides and back, with only enough length on top to comb back in a careless style that made Maya think of drawings of ocean waves breaking against rocky cliffs.

The hair framed a lean, angular, rawboned face with a high forehead and a distinctive shelf of a brow above eyes that were an incredibly bright shade of green, the color of iced jade. And they were fanned by the longest, thickest eyelashes any woman had ever dreamed of for herself.

From there Maya's gaze slid to a nose that was long, thin, ridged in the center and pointed at the tip, with nostrils that didn't match. And yet, as noses went, it was the sexiest one she had ever seen.

He had a roller coaster of a mouth that rose from one deep-dipping corner to a high peak, dropped into a sharp valley of a philtrum, rose again—though not quite as high on the other side—only to curve back to the opposite corner in the most irregular and intriguing way. And all over a lush, full lower lip.

He also had a jawline sharp enough to slice bread, a chin that had only a hint of an indentation, which was a little off center, and great ears—close to his head, not too large, not too small.

All in all, it was hardly a conventionally handsome face, and yet conventional or not, there was no denying that he was ruggedly, staggeringly attractive.

"Name's Shane McDermot," he said by way of introducing himself.

"I know. Now. I mean I just realized it," she answered, showing him the article she'd had a particular interest in.

When he saw it, he screwed up that handsome face into a grimace. "Embarrassing," he said simply.

Maya raised an eyebrow at that. "Seemed pretty flattering to me."

"Makes me sound like nothin' but a side of beef with a bank account."

True enough. But somehow Maya had thought that would please a guy like him.

Then it occurred to her that she didn't have any idea what a "guy like him" was like, and felt ashamed of herself for making assumptions and prejudgments. It was especially unforgivable when she was headed for the job she had signed on to do in Elk Creek.

"You're right," she said by way of apologizing.

"And if this had been written by a man about a woman who had used brains, initiative and hard work to make a success of herself and just happened to look a certain way, I wouldn't blame the woman for shooting the writer."

Shane McDermot smiled at her and it was enough to melt her insides. "I wouldn't go that far. But still I didn't think I was lettin' myself in for so many things like that—or things like that," he added with a nod toward the spot where the woman had been moments before.

Maya could feel her face heating again at the reminder. But she toughed it through. "You mean things like that—" she poked a thumb over her shoulder "—aren't what every man dreams of?"

"Maybe what every teenage boy dreams of," he said wryly. "But I'm a long way from bein' a teenage boy."

A long, glorious way from it.

"Didn't you have any say in what went into this article?"

"Ha! I agreed to give the interview—if you could call it an interview when the reporter was less interested in askin' questions than she was in makin' a date for a late-night romp. But I didn't see what she finally wrote up before it hit the stands. Not that it would have mattered. Freedom of the press, you know. I couldn't have nixed it no matter what." He shook that handsome head and gave a wry laugh. "Well, at least my brother's gonna love it."

"Why is that?"

"We're identical twins and *Prominence Magazine* wanted us to share one of their twelve slots for most eligible bachelor. But my brother didn't want all the fuss he thought it would stir up. I figured a little free publicity was all that would come of it and that it'd be good for business. I thought, what harm could it do? But this time around my brother was right and I underestimated just how much fuss I was in for. Women like that—" once again he pointed his chin to the spot above Maya's head "—and articles like the one in your magazine are about to drive me crazy and Ry will be rubbin' it in to no end."

That seemed to exhaust the subject and bring them to a point where they had to choose either to return to their previous separate pursuits or to go on to make new conversation.

Ordinarily Maya would have reburied her nose in her magazine. But finding herself accidentally in a position to learn a little about the man she'd been sent to assess—before he knew who she was and made an effort to put his best foot forward—seemed like an opportunity she shouldn't ignore. So she decided to use it to best advantage and forge ahead with more conversation.

Glancing at their surroundings, she said, "I wouldn't think a man in your position would be riding a train."

He looked around, too, as if he might have missed something. "Why is that?"

"I'd think business would keep you at a faster pace and you'd want the speed of a private plane or a helicopter."

He leaned slightly forward and pointed a long, thick index finger out the window. "Look over there," he ordered, sounding as if he were confiding something in her.

Maya did as she was told.

"See those three buffalo grazing? And beyond them, that lake that's so clear it glistens? And farther up, where the aspens are just beginnin' to leaf in among the pines on that mountainside… You can't see this kind of scenery from a plane or a helicopter."

It was beautiful, she had to admit. And she'd been missing it by reading that dumb article.

"What about driving? You could have seen it all if you traveled by car."

"But if I travel by car, I end up payin' more attention to my drivin' than to what I'm drivin' through. Besides, there's not anything that matches up to the motion and sound of a train. To me it's like steppin' back in time, slowin' things down so you can appreciate what you should appreciate. In my mind it's right up there with ridin' a horse out on the open range instead of takin' a truck, or helpin' to birth a new calf, or workin' with your bare hands in the earth—it puts you in touch with your roots. And I think that's a good thing."

The note of intimacy in his tone had an unexpected effect on Maya. It lit a spark in her that made her nerve endings spring to life, made her forget for a moment that they were just two strangers on a train, that she was—in essence—doing a job and shouldn't be enjoying herself so much. Or enjoying him so much, either.

She sat back in her seat again.

"What about you?" he asked. "How come you took the train to wherever you're goin'?"

He sounded genuinely interested, and to Maya that was a refreshing change from the men she usually met who thought making conversation meant waiting for her next question so they could talk about themselves some more. She only wished she had as lyrical an answer as he'd given. But she didn't.

"My car is too old to make the trip," she said with a self-deprecating shrug.

Something about that made him grin at her. A grin so engaging it set off inexplicable little twitters of delight in her that had absolutely no business being there.

A voice came over the speaker system just then, announcing Elk Creek as the next stop. Maya breathed a sigh of relief. Maybe she'd do better at this when they met on more formal ground.

Shane McDermot took his Stetson from the vacant seat next to him and straightened from his more relaxed position, pulling in long, jean-clad legs and big cowboy-booted feet, readying himself to disembark. "This is where I get off. But then you probably guessed that," he said with yet another nod at her magazine.

Maya closed it and jammed it into the outer pocket of the suitcase that was her traveling companion. "That's where I'm headed, too," she confessed.

"You're goin' to Elk Creek?" he said with no small amount of surprise.

"Mmm-hmm. I'm on a working vacation."

"*Nobody* vacations in Elk Creek without a reason," he said with a chuckle that was warm enough to feel like a summer's breeze to Maya's heightened senses.

"I'm visiting my mother," she explained without giving him a clue as to the purpose of the *working* part of the trip, since an element of surprise was necessary.

"That so? Who's your mother?"

"Margie Wilson. She owns—"

"Margie Wilson's Café," he finished for her.

"You know her?"

"Sure I know Margie. Everybody does."

And everyone always had. Sometimes in ways that had mortified the young Maya....

"I just didn't know she had a daughter," Shane continued. "Imagine that. I've been livin' in Elk Creek better than ten years and I didn't know. You must keep yourself pretty scarce."

"Mmm," was all Maya would admit.

But the train pulled into the station at that moment, sparing her the need to say more.

"I should have a car waitin' for me. Can I give you a lift?" he offered.

It was tempting and that temptation surprised Maya

because she realized it had to do with a niggling urge not to say goodbye to him just yet. To prolong her time with him, if only for the few minutes it would take to drive from the train station halfway up Elk Creek's main drag—Center Street—to where her mother's restaurant was located.

Not a good sign, she told herself. And for just that reason, she rejected the offer.

"Thanks, but the walk sounds good after sitting for so long."

"Let me at least help you with your bag, then," he said as he stood.

And boy, did he stand!

The man had to be at least two inches over six feet tall, and Maya's eyes did a slow roll the whole way up thick, powerful-looking legs to narrow hips and a V-shaped torso inside a pale yellow shirt that broadened to shoulders a mile wide. He was a tower of pure, potent masculinity that matched his handsome face with every bit as much appeal. So much so that for a moment she was left dumbfounded and he had her suitcase off the seat beside her before she could think to argue.

Then he stepped into the aisle and waited for Maya to step out in front of him.

It took some effort to pull herself together and find her purse, but when she'd managed, she slid out of the tiny section they'd occupied and headed for the exit.

No sooner had she passed the seat that had backed

her own when she heard a woman's voice say, "You sure you aren't interested?"

Maya glanced around in time to see the woman who had bared her breasts earlier. She was standing, facing the aisle, and offering them once more to Shane.

Feeling the heat rise in her face again, Maya wished she had her suitcase in hand so she could make a run for it. But as it was, she could only descend the three steps to get off the train and wait for Shane as she heard him give a quick, firm rejection to the second offer and follow her out.

"Damn," she heard him mutter to himself as he did. "What gets into folks?"

But the question was only rhetorical as he came to stand with Maya on the platform of Elk Creek's old-fashioned train depot with its yellow-and-white-gingerbread station house.

Maya retrieved her suitcase rather than risk being without it if anything else should happen to make her want to disappear in a hurry.

"Thanks," she said as she took it, all too aware of the heat generated from his hand when hers closed around the handle.

"How long will you be in town?" he asked then.

"Hard to say. A little while."

"And if I wanted to look you up, who would I ask for?"

"Oh. I'm sorry. I didn't tell you my name. I'm Maya."

"Wilson? Or is there a married name?"

"No, it's Wilson." And she hated that his interest pleased her so much.

"I'll probably be seein' you, then, Maya Wilson."

"I'm sure." Little did he know…

"And I'll be lookin' forward to it," he said with another of those smiles that were as irregular as his features, lifting higher on one side than the other, but no less charming for its tilt.

And as Maya said goodbye to him and headed down the platform stairs, she thought that she could understand women taking particular notice of him wherever he went—magazine article or no magazine article.

After all, he was terrific-looking, pleasant, self-effacing, courteous and as sexy as they came. There would have to be something wrong with a woman who wasn't affected by the package he presented.

So if she was feeling a tug of attraction to him, it didn't mean anything, she assured herself.

And certainly Shane McDermot being one of the world's most eligible—and appealing—bachelors wouldn't influence her. Not personally. Not professionally. Not in any way.

Except maybe in the way she dragged her feet as she left the vicinity of the train station so she could keep on watching him just as long as it was humanly possible.…

Two

Maya was on Shane's mind as he drove through town and headed for the ranch his grandfather had turned over to the grandchildren ten years ago.

Stunning was how Shane would describe Margie Wilson's daughter. He'd discovered *that* the moment he'd taken the seat across from her on the train.

She had long, sleek hair that fell past her shoulders in a dark, rich cascade the color of Christmas chestnuts. It was cut so precisely there wasn't a single stray end in the whole thick mass, and it shone as vibrantly as French silk.

Her skin was just as flawless. Smooth peaches and cream. Country-girl skin, he thought.

She had a small, perfect nose and lips that looked so soft, so supple, so sweet he'd spent a lot of the train ride distracted from the scenery outside by curiosity about whether or not they felt as good as they looked.

And when that other woman had popped up behind Maya's seat and Maya had finally raised her gaze from her magazine to actually look at him, he'd had at least one desire fulfilled—he'd gotten to see her eyes.

He hadn't been disappointed. Oh, no, not disappointed at all. Her eyes were great big doe eyes, so dark they were nearly black. Radiant. Luminous. Beautiful.

And shocked to see what they'd seen behind her.

That creamy skin had flushed an incredibly becoming pink, delighting him no end. After too many encounters with women as tactless, tasteless and downright tacky as the one on the train, Maya's blush had been as refreshing as springwater.

That was when he'd started thinking she looked familiar, Shane thought as he drove past Jackson Heller's ranch and then the large Culhane property, which now included two ranches, since the Culhane brothers had married the sisters next door to their place. But not until Maya had told him she was Margie Wilson's daughter had he realized what made her seem familiar.

Margie Wilson's daughter…

That had been a surprise. For no particular reason other than that he'd never seen Margie with any kin. Shane had just assumed she was alone in the world. Funny that no one had ever mentioned a daughter. Especially one as breathtaking as Maya.

And she *was* breathtaking. So breathtaking he hadn't been able to take his eyes off her.

He wondered if Margie had looked like that in her younger days. She was a handsome older woman, there was no doubt about that. But had she been as striking as her daughter?

Hard to tell.

Margie was bigger than Maya. Wider, heavier, taller by a couple of inches, because he would estimate that

Maya only topped out at about five foot four to Margie's five-six or so. And Maya was compact. Not too thin, but certainly not fat. Pleasantly proportioned with only enough curves to make her undeniably a woman. A woman a man could pull up against him and know from the soft feel that he had something feminine in his arms.

And when she smiled, he thought, that was something to see. It lit up her whole face. It put a sparkle into those dark eyes. It showed straight white teeth. And it had set off a little electrical charge deep inside him that had had a lot more effect than that other woman's bare breasts. A whole lot more effect.

An effect he hadn't experienced in a while.

He'd have to watch that if he met up with her again. Instinct warned him that Maya Wilson was a woman who put him at risk for letting down his guard.

And that was not something he wanted to do. Especially not with someone who had been reading that fluff magazine article about him. Someone who had had the response he'd seen in her when she connected him to it—she'd bought into that beefcake nonsense hook, line and sinker.

Although to be fair, she had understood his point of view on being depicted like that.

But still, he thought as he turned off the main road onto the gravel drive that led to his house, at first she hadn't figured him for anything more than the article presented, and he knew too well that it was damn near impossible to get people to look beyond the surface if that was all they were inclined to see. And there was no way of telling yet if that *was* what she was inclined to see. So he had to be cautious. Same as always. Or at least the same as he'd learned the hard way to be four years ago.

The house came into view just then and he forced his thoughts away from Maya. It was no easy task, but he focused on the welcoming sight of home, checking out the new roof and rain gutters he and Ry had scheduled to be put on while he was away.

The remodeling and additions to the house his grandparents had lived in for more than fifty years were seamless. The original structure was now not much more than an entrance to the rest of the house, but Shane, Ry and their three other siblings—who all shared actual ownership of the ranch even if they didn't live and work there—had wanted to retain it for their grandfather's sake. None of them had liked the idea of obliterating what the old man had built with his own two hands, even though Buzz had said it didn't matter.

Beyond the five hundred square feet of clapboard blossomed the twelve thousand square feet of addition—a sprawling, single-story white structure with Tudor overtones in the high-pitched roof, the large-paned glass windows and the pointed eaves.

The front porch eased like a handlebar mustache into covered verandas on both sides of the newer portion where the bedroom wings spread out from the east and west. The wings were made up of three suites each, every suite containing a bedroom, bathroom and sitting room with its own French doors to the outside. The object was for the five McDermot siblings to have private areas of the house from which they could come and go whenever they pleased and without using the main entrance. The sixth suite had been intended as a guest room but now had a permanent occupant.

Shane pulled around to the eight-car garage that had been converted from the barn when the newer, larger and decidedly more contemporary counterpart had been erected last summer. He parked inside and then walked around the pool, which was due to be filled just before Memorial Day, stepped onto the redwood deck and skirted the hot tub to cross to the back of the house, where six more sets of French doors made up the kitchen's rear wall and allowed the house to be almost completely opened up to the deck in the summer.

He unlocked one set of doors in the center and went into a restaurant-size—and equipped—kitchen with a warm country-oak motif that kept it from looking stark and industrial. Nothing was going on there and the house was quiet except for the far-off murmur of a television.

Wondering where everyone was, Shane checked the time. Four o'clock. Ry probably hadn't yet finished up work for the day, but usually Junebug was in the kitchen starting supper by now. Shane went from the kitchen into the dining room—taking the long way through the great room because he was curious about where Junebug might be. But he still didn't spot his housekeeper, so he turned to the right and entered the hall that led to the bedrooms on the west side of the house.

"Hey, Buzz, you old bear, where are you?" he called as he neared the room from which the television noise was coming.

"Humph, where d'ya think I am?" a gruff voice answered just as Shane reached the doorway of the frontmost suite.

That was as far as he went into the room. He leaned a shoulder against the jamb, folded his arms over his chest and one ankle over the other so he could take a look at the elderly man ensconced in the middle of the king-size bed.

Buzz—as everyone called Bertrum Martindale— was sitting on top of the covers, wearing an old, sweat-stained Stetson hat. It had fit years ago when he'd carried more weight and muscle, but now it dwarfed him. He also had on a tank-style undershirt that exposed a sunken chest and arms that seemed covered in chicken skin, boxer shorts with the Tasmanian Devil cartoon character emblazoned all over them, an elaborate brace on his right knee, which extended upward to mid-scrawny-thigh and downward to mid-bony-calf, and a pair of cowboy boots so aged the toes were curled like elf slippers.

Shane couldn't suppress a smile. "I'll bet you sent Junebug out of here screamin' about that hat and those boots, didn't you?" he guessed.

"Old woman," Buzz grumbled, as if that were indictment enough.

"She's nowhere around. If I hadn't shown up, she might've left you here stewin' with no supper tonight."

"Ha! She'da git her tail back after a time and we both know it. Just went off in a snit. Got no sense, that old woman. Know's nothin' 'bout the male of the species. If she did, she'd know a man's got a right to his hat and his boots when he has a mind fer 'em."

"In bed?"

"Even in bed."

"Junebug raised six sons. How is it you think she doesn't know about men?"

"It's a wonder they weren't all sissies when she liked to git through with 'em."

Shane knew there was no winning this argument. His grandfather and his housekeeper enjoyed their fights too much to ever be persuaded the other might be right about anything.

Instead of trying, Shane pointed his chin at his grandfather's knee. "How's the leg comin' along?"

"Better. I'll be out on the range with you 'fore long."

"Is the nurse lettin' you walk on it yet?"

"Soon. That's all she'll say. Real soon."

"Hurtin' you much?"

Buzz just shrugged shoulders that had shrunk from their younger selves. He wouldn't admit to being in pain even if he was, and Shane knew it.

"Anything excitin' happen around here while I was gone?"

"Humph. Women."

"You mean women other than Junebug and your nurse?"

"Yessiree, I do. All kinds of females comin' 'round lookin' for you. Ry says he shoulda tied you up and left you in the barn so's you couldn't go'n do that eligible bachelor thing. It's wreakin' havoc."

Shane made a face as if someone had thrown water at him. "More women have been comin' around?"

"At least a half dozen just since you've been gone."

"I was hopin' things had died down."

"Ha! Died down my Aunt Fanny! One of 'em got in through my winder and climbed right here into bed with me in the middle of the night. Pert near liked to mo-lest me 'fore she figered out it wasn't you. Then when Ry come chargin' in, she thought he was you and she was all over him, too. Had to call the sheriff and have him haul her away because she wouldn't go on her own, nohow. Ry had to put locks on all the winders day after that."

"You must be gettin' old," Shane teased him, "if a woman climbed into your bed and you didn't know what to do with her except call for Ry."

"I knew what to do with her all right. But Ry, he heard me askin' who the hell she was and he come in like a bull and yanked her out 'fore I had a chance. If she'da got a taste of me she'da forgot all about you."

Shane laughed, knowing his grandfather was full of hot air more than anything. "Maybe we could find out from the sheriff who she was and get her back here for you."

"Long's she don't mind a man wearin' his boots to bed," Buzz played along. Then he said, "How was your trip?"

"Interestin'. Met an Elk Creek girl on the train on the way home."

"That so? One you never met before?"

"Margie Wilson's daughter."

"Maya."

"You know her?"

"Knew her when she was a kid. Same as everybody knows everybody 'round these parts."

"How come I never heard about Margie havin' a daughter?"

"Were you s'pose to? She left town 'fore you ever showed up."

"Just seems curious."

"Or you are, you mean," Buzz said slyly. "Liked 'er, did ya, boy?"

"She was nice enough," Shane admitted cautiously.

"Grew up lookin' mighty good, too, as I recall."

"That she did."

"She here visitin' Margie?"

"That and doin' some kind of job. She said it was a workin' vacation but she didn't say what kind of work she'd be doin'. You know what she does for a livin'?"

"Never did hear, no. Why? You want to hire her for somethin', do you?" Buzz goaded, just the way Shane had goaded Buzz moments earlier about the woman in his bed.

"Wasn't thinkin' anything at all except to wonder what business she had in Elk Creek."

"Yeah, sure," the old man said dubiously. "I'll bet you got a hankerin' fer this one, elsewise, why'd you be sniffin' 'round 'bout her?"

Shane grinned at his grandfather. "I told you she was nice enough," he said simply as he pushed off the doorjamb, unwilling to say more about Maya. "I'd better see if I can't smooth the waters with Junebug and get us some supper cooked tonight."

"Gonna see 'er agin?"

"Who? Junebug? I better, or how else am I goin' to get us somethin' to eat?"

"I didn't mean Junebug. I meant Margie Wilson's daughter and you know it."

Seeing Maya again was an appealing thought. Too appealing. But Shane wouldn't commit to more than, "Elk Creek's a small town. I'll probably run into her."

"At least yer hopin' so."

Shane merely smiled and headed down the hall in the direction of the kitchen.

But his grandfather was right, he realized along the way. He *was* hoping to meet up with Maya again. Hoping and maybe even thinking in the back of his mind how he could manage it.

Not that he'd do anything about it if he had any sense, he told himself. But already, after no more than half an hour since he'd left her, the desire to see her again was strong.

Mighty strong.

Surprisingly strong.

Shane shook his head in amazement at just how strong it was, wondering about himself. And wondering if maybe somewhere on that train ride, he'd lost what sense he did have....

Elk Creek, Wyoming.

Some of the best times of Maya's life had occurred here, she thought as she walked down Center Street in the direction of her mother's restaurant. Of course, some of the worst times had also happened here, so she always came back to the small town with mixed feelings.

The best times had been early on, when she'd been a young child, and now, seeing carefree kids riding their bicycles along the brick-paved sidewalks in front of the quaint, well-tended shops made her remember the good.

Maya recalled lazy summer afternoons when the fire department had opened up the hydrants to let the younger residents cool off in the spray. And evenings when she and her friends would lie on the lush green grass of the town square, which was surrounded by the tall redbrick courthouse and the white steepled church and the medical center that was really only a big old converted house, and watch fireflies until bedtime without a single adult to add restraints. And lemonade stands had always paid off.

Winters were full of ice-skating and sledding. Of kids being enlisted to help decorate all the trees in the town square for the Christmas holidays. Of hayrides and bonfires—and s'mores made from marshmallows toasted over the flames. Of being welcome to stop in at just about any home or business en route to a friend's house on a cold day when fingers, toes and noses got too chilled—and usually being offered hot chocolate before going out again.

Elk Creek was a place she had thought she would never want to leave. At least she'd thought that for most of her years growing up there.

Until the worst of times had hit. Then she'd changed her mind.

"Maya? Is that you?"

Maya was only a few feet from the old-fashioned general store when she spotted Kansas Daye—Kansas *Heller* now—stepping outside with a watering can in hand. Kansas had taken over the store from her folks when they'd retired. She and Maya had been good friends—best friends—all the years they'd gone to school together.

"It's me," Maya answered. Kansas was the one person she made a point of seeing when she came to town. The only one she sought out purposely. Although this trip, Maya hadn't been too sure she would do that. Not now that Kansas was married to a Heller.

But there was Kansas, watering flowers that looked newly planted around the base of the Victorian street lamp that was identical to those that lined the full length of Center Street on both sides.

"I didn't know you were coming for a visit. Shame on you for not writing or calling to tell me."

"It was sort of a last-minute thing," Maya said.

That wasn't entirely true. She'd known about the trip for ten days—plenty of time to have made a simple phone call to Kansas. But she let the statement stand rather than admit the truth. She wasn't willing to explain that if she had to dodge Kansas in order to maintain a distance from her friend's husband or any of the rest of his family, that was what she intended to do.

"How long will you be in town?" Kansas asked.

"I'm not sure. I have some things to take care of."

"Through Mother's Day on Sunday, though, I'll bet."

"Definitely through Mother's Day."

"Great! Then I'm hereby recruiting you for the Mother's Day dinner in the church basement."

"I don't know about that...."

"I won't let you refuse. You're always sneaking into town and then sneaking back out again without seeing anybody but your mother or me, and then she and I are left to answer to everybody who would have liked to say hello to you. This is perfect. Practically the whole town turns out so you'll get to see everybody. The men cook and it's a hoot. I won't take no for an answer.''

"I'll leave it up to Mom," Maya conceded reluctantly. "But if she'd rather we spend the day alone—"

"She won't. She always comes. The big communal dinner makes the day extra special and really gives moms the time off.''

"I'll talk to her," Maya said, still hedging and hoping her mother wouldn't want to go.

"But you'll give me a call before then, won't you? So we can get together?" Kansas asked.

"Sure," Maya agreed with no more enthusiasm than she'd had for the Mother's Day dinner. She wondered if she could persuade Kansas to meet somewhere other than Kansas's house for their get-together this time around. Somewhere Linc Heller was not likely to show up.

"I better get over to the diner now. Mom's expecting me," she said, before Kansas could pin her down to anything more.

Kansas gave her an impromptu hug. "I'm so glad you're here. You don't come home often enough.''

"I'll see you soon," was Maya's only answer as she returned her friend's hug and walked on.

Maya's first sight of the restaurant her mother owned and operated warmed her heart. It was an inviting place with a big picture window out front, decorated with tied-back, ruffled white curtains that made it look like a country kitchen. The sign above the door, which proclaimed it Margie Wilson's Café, was a hand-painted oval with the words arched over a stencil of a pot of calico flowers.

A bell clattered when Maya opened the door—a farmhouse door with a cross-board bottom and nine panes of glass in the top—and she stepped into the scent of freshly baked yeast rolls and cinnamon-apple pie.

It was too early yet for the supper crowd. The tables that were all covered in red-and-white-checked cloths were empty and only a lone man sat on one of the cushioned stools at the counter, eating a slice of triple-layer chocolate cake and drinking a cup of coffee.

A teenage waitress Maya didn't recognize approached her, but before the girl could say anything, Maya said, "I'm Margie's daughter. I'll bet she's in the kitchen, isn't she?"

The girl nodded and returned to setting silverware rolls at the place settings of a table that seemed to have just been cleaned.

Maya made her way along the aisle beside the booths that lined one wall and peered over the swinging doors that always reminded her of a western saloon. Her mother was sliding a huge pan of her famous chicken-and-dumpling casserole into the industrial-size oven.

"Hi, Mom," she said as if she'd just happened by.

Margie shot a glance in her direction, closed the oven door with the hem of her white apron and made a beeline for Maya as Maya stepped into the heat of the kitchen.

"I was beginning to wonder if I should go looking for you. I heard the train arrive more than half an hour ago," Margie said, pulling her daughter into a hug not unlike the one Kansas had given her moments before.

"I had a little bit of a holdup getting off the train and I stopped to talk to Kansas," Maya explained, returning the hug.

"Let me look at you," Margie said, holding Maya at arm's length. The two of them were close even though Maya rarely came to Elk Creek. Instead, Margie visited her in Cheyenne, enjoying the city and the chance to get away, and they talked on the telephone every other day. But it had been nearly three months since Margie had been to Cheyenne, so she took a long look at Maya.

"I like your hair a little shorter," she said when she'd completed the tour. "I didn't think I would, but I do. I never realized how much more sophisticated it would look just below your shoulders, or how country-bumpkinish it made you seem when you wore it to your waist."

Maya laughed. "Thanks. I'm glad to know I've looked like a country bumpkin all these years."

Margie looked the same. She was one of those women whose face aged well because her bone structure was so good. Even the extra pounds she had put on over time hadn't marred that. Her hair was salt-and-pepper gray, cut very short so she didn't have to wear a hair net in the kitchen. Her eyes were the same dark brown of Maya's eyes, and her skin—though lined—was luscious. It was no wonder, Maya thought, that Shag Heller had been smitten with her.

"Come on in and sit on the stool while I get the potatoes whipped and a few other things ready for the rush. Then we can go. Mary Ellen is coming in at five-thirty to take over so we can have the evening to ourselves. Want coffee or tea or something?"

"No, thanks," Maya answered as she set her bags on the floor, out of the way of the swinging doors, and pulled the wooden stool she'd perched on even as a kid over to the huge worktable in the center of the room.

"So what was the holdup getting off the train?" Margie asked.

"One of those it's-a-small-world things. My seat-mate from Cheyenne was Shane McDermot. Although I didn't know it until we were just about here." Maya went on to tell her mother how she'd met Shane and why their departure had been slowed, without adding that her stroll from the train station hadn't been any too speedy because she'd been intent on keeping sight of him for as long as she could.

"Now, there's a man who could take good care of a woman," Margie said when she had finished.

Maya had a sudden flash of that big, muscular cow-boy's body taking care of needs no mother would talk about with her daughter. Needs, Maya was certain, that were different from anything her mother had in mind. Needs she had to put some effort into getting her mind off, once the seeds had been planted.

"Funny that he's lived in Elk Creek for so long and I've never met him before," Maya said to distract herself from her wandering thoughts.

"It isn't funny at all. You hardly ever come home, and when you do, it's only for a few days at a time. And you spend those alone with me, even though I tell you and tell you to go out and see some old friends besides Kansas. Now you know what you've been missing," Margie said pointedly.

"When I come to Elk Creek, I come to see you. I haven't wanted to see anybody else. Except Kansas."

"Until now," Margie said as if she could see right through Maya. "Maybe now that you're interested in Shane McDermot you'll change your mind."

"Interested? Who said anything about being interested in Shane McDermot?"

"Nobody had to say it. I can see it," Margie said, as pleased as if she'd just watched her daughter take her first step.

"I'm only interested in Shane McDermot insofar as he is taking care of his grandfather and has become one of my cases."

Margie laughed. "Now I know he tweaked your interest. Anytime you use words like 'insofar as,' I know you're covering up something. And you *should* be interested in him. He'd be a good catch for a single girl like you. You know what I always say—better to be a rich man's treasure than a poor man's slave."

Maya flinched at that statement and wondered how,

with the way things had worked out in her mother's life, Margie could still say something like that.

But that wasn't a subject they talked about.

Instead Maya stood up. "You know what? Since you're tied up here for a while yet, I think maybe I'll take a run out to the McDermot ranch right now. I was going to wait until tomorrow, but with the way talk travels around here, they're liable to hear something about what I do for a living and put two and two together. And this first visit needs to be a surprise."

"Good idea," Margie agreed in a tone that told Maya she didn't for a minute believe her daughter was only trying to do her job. Clearly Margie was convinced it was an excuse to see Shane McDermot again. "Strike while the iron is hot," Margie added, as if to prove Maya's suspicions.

Maya rolled her eyes but didn't say anything. It was a waste of breath attempting to convince her mother that she had only a professional visit in mind. So instead she said, "Can I take your car?"

"It's out back. Keys are in it."

"I won't be long. This will just be a quick spot check and an introduction, and then I'll be back and we can go home."

"Don't worry about that. I can walk home when I'm ready to go. And if you don't make it till late— well, I'll understand."

Once again Margie's tone was full of innuendo. But this time Maya felt inclined to deny what her mother was insinuating.

"This is work, Mom. It's what I came to do, re-member?"

"Mmm-hmm…" Margie murmured knowingly.

"There's nothing personal to it and that's how I want it. How it has to be."

"Mmm-hmm…"

"I'll be back in an hour, tops."

"Don't hurry on my account."

"I'll be back in an hour because that's all the longer it will take me to do my job," Maya insisted.

"Mmm-hmm…"

Changing Margie's mind was hopeless so Maya quit trying. "See you in a bit," was all she said as she took her suitcase and crossed the kitchen to the restaurant's rear door, and exited into the alley that ran behind it.

This *was* a purely professional visit, she told herself as she set the suitcase on the back seat of her mother's car and then got behind the wheel. No matter what Margie thought.

And that was how she wanted it. Purely professional. Nothing personal to it at all.

On the other hand, Maya was glad her mother couldn't know that her heart was racing and something much too akin to excitement was rushing through her veins at the thought of seeing Shane again. And professional or personal, the reason didn't seem to matter.

In the eleven years since Maya had left Elk Creek she'd never once driven outside of town during a visit back. So what she found as she left the city proper and entered the surrounding countryside surprised her. Things had changed.

There were additions and improvements to almost every house she drove past—each one some distance from the other because ranches stretched far and wide.

But nothing was as much of a shock as her first sight of the old Martindale place. The *McDermot* place now.

Where once there had been a small home, there stood what had to have been the biggest house in the whole county—a beautiful place that looked as if it should be set amid an English garden.

Clearly the magazine article she'd read on the train hadn't exaggerated Shane McDermot's wealth if he was able to afford this grand a house, Maya thought.

Margie kept her informed on Elk Creek news— whether she wanted to be kept informed or not—so she knew that Shane McDermot and his brother had taken over the ranch after a long family feud had been resolved. One of the town's long-standing tales was of how Buzz Martindale hadn't approved of the man his young daughter had eloped with and so had been estranged from her for years.

But at about the same time Maya had left Elk Creek, a reconciliation had taken place between Buzz and his daughter that reunited the family, complete with five grown grandchildren. Shortly after that, Buzz had turned the ranch over to those grandchildren—although only Shane and his twin had left Texas to come to Elk Creek—and moved with his wife to a suburb of Denver.

Maya recalled her mother talking over the last several years about the new, bigger house the McDermots were building. But either Margie's descriptions had been lacking or Maya hadn't been listening, because she'd had no idea that a sprawling estate house was what had gone up out there.

Seeing it now made the circumstances that had led to her visit all the more curious.

According to the report that had come across her desk, Buzz's wife had died two years ago and he'd stayed on in the small apartment the two of them had shared since leaving Elk Creek.

Six weeks ago Buzz had fallen and broken his knee. The condition in which the paramedics who answered his 911 call had found him and the information the hospital had managed to glean from talking to him, as well as the physical signs he'd exhibited of undernourishment, had prompted hospital personnel to call in Social Services. Social Services, in conjunction with the hospital staff, had felt Buzz was no longer able to care for himself or live on his own.

Apparently only Shane and his brother lived on the Elk Creek ranch full-time, but they had stepped in at that point, bringing Buzz back to the small town rather than allowing him to be placed in a nursing home. That's when it had become Maya's assignment to look in on the arrangement, to make sure that the old man was not left on his own and that he was being adequately cared for.

What she wondered as she followed the horseshoe-curved drive around a mammoth sculptured waterfall that looked like an artist's rendition of a natural rock formation was why, when his grandsons were out here living like this, Buzz had been alone in a small apartment in the first place.

But it wasn't her job to make prejudgments, she reminded herself as she got out of the car and headed up to the front door.

As she rang the bell, it occurred to her that the entrance portion of the house was the original homestead. The door itself was now two doors that opened in the center and had elaborate stained-glass ovals in their top halves. And what once had been the Martindale home blended so smoothly into the new structure that if she didn't already know it had stood for decades, she would never have guessed that it hadn't been erected at the same time as the remainder of the building.

When Maya heard the door open in answer to the bell, she reined in her study of the place. Expecting to find a maid or butler ready to admit her, she raised her gaze instead all the way up the long length of Shane McDermot himself.

"Well, hey," he said with a surprised lilt to his voice as he slid one hand up the door's edge and shifted his weight onto his right hip in a relaxed pose that was sexier than Maya wished it was. "I didn't think I'd be seein' you so soon."

She knew what he was thinking. It was there in the tone of his voice, in the pleased and slightly smug expression on his face. He thought she was just another woman chasing after him—like the one on the train, only with her plain white blouse still in place.

Maya bristled at the assumption and hurried to alter the impression. "I know you were informed by Social Services in Denver that there would be impromptu home visits from a caseworker to check on Buzz and see how things were going here," she said, rather than answering his greeting.

"And you're the caseworker?" he guessed before she could say any more.

"And I'm the caseworker."

"I'll be damned. So we're the workin' part of this trip for you?"

"Afraid so."

His gorgeous features still looked pleased, though the smugness disappeared as that supple mouth of his eased into an ornery smile. "Afraid? Nothin' to be afraid of here."

"It was only a figure of speech." And he was wrong—there *was* something to be afraid of here. Him. Or at least the fact that merely standing a few feet away from him was enough to do sparkling things to her insides.

He straightened away from the door and stepped

back. "Come on in, Ms. Caseworker, and explain to me what this involves."

What it wasn't supposed to involve was her pulse racing faster than it had earlier or the sudden increase in her awareness of every little thing about the man. Like the careless way his hair waved back on top. Or how bright green his eyes were. Or how big he was— big and hard-muscled enough to make images flash through her mind of what it would feel like to move up close to him, to have his powerful-looking arms wrap around her, to snake her own arms under his and lay her palms against his back as she pressed her cheek to his chest....

Maya shook herself slightly to escape the instant fantasy that had played itself out so suddenly in her mind. He'd asked her what the home visits entailed, she reminded herself as she cleared her throat. "I'll need to see Buzz, talk to him, see where he is and if he's able to get around safely. I'll need to know who looks after him, if he's ever alone and for how long. Just generally what his living and care arrangements are, how he's doing, how everyone in the household feels about the situation, things like that."

"And here I thought this was a social call," he teased, sounding charmingly disappointed.

"What you thought was that I was just another woman on a manhunt for you," she heard herself say wryly before she knew the words were going to come out.

But he didn't take offense. He grinned, showing her

straight white teeth as intriguing and appealing as the rest of him.

"Maybe that's just what I was hopin'." His green eyes did a slow roll down her body and back up again, making her feel hot all over for no reason she could fathom. When his gaze returned to her face, his grin widened even further. "So, does this mean you're not gonna pull up your shirt for me?"

Okay, she'd had that coming. She was the one who'd brought up women throwing themselves at him. But she could still feel her face suffusing with color. "That's what it means, all right."

"Shame," he murmured, obviously enjoying her discomfort.

Maya cleared her throat again and attempted once more to get down to business. "I just thought I'd make a quick drop-in now to say hi to Buzz and—"

"And check us out when you know we haven't had time to spruce anything up because I just got here," he supplied for her without any of the rancor some people felt when they suddenly found themselves under scrutiny in situations like this.

"I'm sorry if it seems intrusive—"

"Folks come and go 'round here all the time. It's no big deal. Especially since we don't have anything to hide. Where would you like to start? Want the grand tour? Or do you want to see Buzz? Or can we just have a sit down, you and I, alone together?"

Just when she thought he'd conceded to behaving himself and treating her visit seriously, his last comment was said with a lascivious quirk of his left eyebrow that let her know he was still putting her on to some degree.

That quirk of his eyebrow also caught her attention, because for the first time she realized that the brow's shape was slightly different from the right one. A small scar was buried in the center of it, shooting toward his eye like a tiny lightning bolt that was barely visible unless he raised his brow.

Maya put some effort into containing her curiosity and her appreciation for the sexy sight that quirky brow presented, once again seizing work as her escape from her wandering attention. She pretended not to have heard the suggestiveness in his tone. "I'm available for counseling if you're having some difficulty adjusting to your grandfather living with you, if that's what you'd like to sit down and talk about."

"If I make out like any of that's true, will I get you all to myself?"

She was beginning to see that he had an incorrigible streak in him and she tried not to like it—as hard as she tried not to feel flattered by his flirting.

"We can have counseling sessions if you feel you need them, yes," she reiterated in a businesslike voice, again acting as if she hadn't caught his real meaning. "As for now, if you'd just show me to Buzz's room, we can save the grand tour for another time—since it is late in the day."

"You'll have to come into the house to get to his room," Shane said then, a laugh in his tone that made

Maya realize she hadn't accepted his invitation to step inside. She was still standing very stiffly, very primly on the landing like a Girl Scout selling cookies.

"Want me to leave the door open so you can make a run for it if you need to?" he teased.

Maya was not a rookie at this, and even when she had been, she'd never felt as awkward as she did at that moment. Something about this man had her off kilter. In more ways than one.

But she didn't want him to know it, so she stepped across the threshold as if he'd just then asked her in. As she did, she caught a whiff of a spicy aftershave that set something fluttering within her, taking her off guard with her sudden, purely instinctive response to it.

Maybe what the man had, she thought, was an animal magnetism that left every woman helpless against the potency of his appeal. Or maybe somewhere in the travels the magazine article had alluded to, he'd come across a magic potion that made him irresistible.

In yet another effort to effect some immunity, Maya focused on the house she'd just entered as Shane closed the door behind her.

She'd been in the Martindale home on only a few occasions as a child, tagging along with her mother to a church or committee meeting. But she hadn't been there often enough to recall exactly what the place had looked like before this new incarnation.

What she did know as she stood in the expansive foyer was that walls had been removed, so that what had been a living room to the right and a den to the left was now just one big open area. It flowed into a great room that had obliterated the old kitchen to accommodate the addition.

From the entryway she could see that the great room was huge. It was well decorated in a warm, rustic fashion that gave the illusion of being a mountain cabin, but it was evident no expense had been spared. Beyond that, it was too far away and—at that moment—too dimly lit to see any of the details.

Shane pointed a thumb toward the hall to one side of the foyer, ignoring the identical corridor opposite it, which she assumed led to the other wing of the house.

The hall he escorted her into stretched for what seemed like blocks and was wide enough to have driven a car through. It was illuminated by discreet skylights in the ceiling that cast what was left of the day's sunshine into the space.

"He's in the first room here," Shane said to her. Then, as he knocked and opened the door, he called into the room, "Got company, Buzz."

The television had been making a faint noise before but was silenced just as Maya stepped into a bedroom the size of her entire apartment in Cheyenne.

It was decorated with a southwestern influence in the handwoven rug hanging on the wall, the white oak armoire, bureau and entertainment center, and the Indian pottery and paintings displayed here and there to add warmth. A sitting room adjoined it, furnished to match and looking more elaborate than Maya's own living room at home. The things that stood out in either room were the hospital bed in the center of the bedroom and the spindly old man propped up on top of it, looking as if he'd fit in better on a cot in a bunkhouse.

She couldn't help but notice that he was dressed in cowboy boots, an undershirt and a pair of Tasmanian Devil undershorts, with what was left of his sparse white hair standing on end around an overly pink scalp. But even though Buzz Martindale was only a shrunken shadow of his former self, Maya recognized him instantly.

And for his part, there was obviously nothing wrong with his eyesight or his memory, because he knew who she was with a single glance.

"Maya Wilson!" he exclaimed, as if he couldn't be more delighted to see her. Then, with a wink at Shane, he said, "This here's Maya Wilson, boy."

"Yep. Know that," Shane answered with another of those laughs in his voice, leading Maya to believe he'd already told his grandfather they'd met on the train and that the two of them were sharing a private joke at her expense.

Shane leaned a shoulder against the doorjamb and Maya moved to the bed. Intent on ignoring him and concentrating on Buzz, she turned her back to Shane and faced the elderly man, hitching a hip onto the edge of his bed to sit down.

"I'm the caseworker Social Services sent to look in on you," she explained.

"That so? You're my watchdog, huh?"

"I guess you could say that."

"Here to do my biddin', make sure I'm bein' treated proper."

"Here to make sure you're being treated properly, yes."

"Then would you git that there hat over on the dresser for me?"

It seemed like a harmless request, so Maya did as he asked. She didn't know what she expected him to do with it, but somehow she hadn't thought he'd put it on his balding head.

"You're gonna tick Junebug off again," Shane's deep voice reminded from behind.

Buzz made a sound that was somewhere between a snort and a satisfied chuckle.

"Is Junebug Brimley looking after you?" Maya asked, opting to ignore the previous exchange between Buzz and Shane.

"Humph. If that's what you want to call it."

"Now, hold up there, Buzz," Shane warned more sternly. "This woman is here in an official capacity to make sure you're bein' well taken care of. Don't go lettin' Maya think you aren't just because Junebug doesn't want you wearin' your hat and boots in bed. If you do your skinny rump is apt to end up in a nursing home where you aren't gonna taste roasted chicken like Junebug's cookin' up right now."

Buzz frowned at his grandson, then said to Maya in a confidential tone, ''Junebug's doin' the cookin' and the cleanin' and the fetchin', and she's doin' a fine job of it, if you don't count how contrary she is. But if you tell 'er I said anythin' good 'bout 'er, I'll hafta call you a liar.''

Maya suppressed a smile at the cantankerous old man and went on to ask a few more simple questions about how he felt, how his knee was healing and what his days involved.

He answered them all, lowering his voice to hushed tones whenever he had something positive to say about Junebug, as if she might overhear, and peppering his conversation with a heavy dose of innocent flirting until Maya concluded that time and age hadn't changed the Buzz she'd always known—he was still jovial, happily ornery, roughly charming and funny.

''So how 'bout you, little Maya?'' he asked after she'd told him they'd covered enough ground for the time being. ''You spoken for yet?''

''No, I'm not spoken for yet,'' she said with a laugh.

''Not married or engaged or nothin'?'' he persisted, eyeing Shane as he did.

''Nothin','' she parroted.

''And will you be makin' more of these here visits?''

''For a while I will be. Just to make sure how you're doing and how your being here is going.''

''I'm thinkin' that you can't be sure if they're feed-in' me good 'nuff 'less you come to dinner one night, though,'' he said like a wily old fox.

"That's true," Shane tossed in from behind her. He hadn't said two words since his warning to his grandfather not to make Junebug out to be a villain, Maya noted. "How 'bout tomorrow night? Say seven?" he suggested, making his grandfather grin.

"These are supposed to be impromptu visits, not visits by invitation," Maya said. "Besides, I know Junebug's a good cook. She worked at the diner a few years back when Mom was sick. I'm sure you're being well fed. The question is, are you eating it and gaining any weight."

"Talk to the nurse 'bout the weight part. But come see for yerself if I'm eatin' or not. Tomorrow night. Seven. I'll even put on some pants," Buzz promised.

"That makes it an offer nobody should refuse," Shane contributed.

But Maya still kept her glance on Buzz. "I'll talk to the nurse about your weight," was all she would commit to.

She said goodbye and patted Buzz's hand where it rested on the mattress. But he flipped it over and caught her hand to keep her from moving. Then he poked his cheek with the index finger of his free hand. "Give an old buzzard a little kiss. Been a long time since I been kissed by a girl pretty as you."

Maya laughed and gave him a light peck on the cheek. "Now, behave yourself," she ordered. "And don't give poor Junebug too much trouble and make her quit. She's just what you need.''

''Humph,'' was his only answer as he let go of her hand to pull his hat down over his face. He laid his head back on the pillows as if he were about to nap against a rock in the desert and effectively dismissed Maya.

She stood and turned to face Shane again. He pushed off the jamb with one broad shoulder, his hands in the rear pockets of his jeans.

''So how'd we do? Did we pass your inspection?'' he asked as he walked her out.

''Like I told Buzz, everything looks good so far. Your home—what I've seen of it—seems not only adequate but pretty incredible.''

''Ready to see the rest?''

''Another time. It's getting late and I've done enough for this first visit. I am curious about something, though,'' she said as they reached the front door.

''What?''

''With all that you have here, why was Buzz in a shabby apartment all alone?''

''Because he's a stubborn old mule. Or didn't you know that? He turned the ranch over to me and Ry and the rest of us kids when my grandmother's asthma got so bad it was dangerous for them not to live closer to a hospital. That's when they moved to Denver—to be near National Jewish, because it's the best place for lung ailments. When Gram died we tried to get Buzz to come back here, but he dug in his heels. He said we didn't need an old coot hangin' 'round our necks like a noose and he wouldn't budge no matter what we did. Ry and I saw the way he was livin' in that apartment, saw that he wasn't eatin' the way he should have been, that he couldn't keep the place up. But he wouldn't let us do anything, and every time I hired somebody to help him he chased them away—the last time with his shotgun. We had plans to kidnap him to get him home when he took that fall. It made it easier on us that you *authorities* told him he had to live with us or go to a nursing home.''

Maya knew Buzz well enough to know it sounded like him and she was relieved to learn that his grandsons had wanted him home even before the accident. Though why it should feel so personally pleasing to her, she didn't understand.

"Well, I'm glad he's here now," she said. Then she added, "And I guess that's about it for me tonight."

Shane was standing between her and the door, a position she thought he'd placed himself in so he could open the door for her. But he didn't make any move and instead just stood there, blocking her way out.

"So, do I get the same perks my grandfather does?"

"Perks?"

He poked a thick finger at his cheek just the way Buzz had.

"I've known Buzz all my life. He used to trade kisses on the cheek for lollipops when I was a kid," she said, as if that served to explain her actions and refuse his request all at once.

"If I go find a lollipop, do I get a kiss, then?"

"You just like giving me a hard time, don't you?"

He grinned. "I'm enjoyin' the hell out of it. Never did see anybody who blushes quite as nice as you do."

"Mmm. Well, I think you've had enough fun for one day and my mother is waiting for me."

Shane just went on smiling down at her, his green eyes alight, and poked his cheek again. "Consider it a toll."

What she was considering was how it might affect her to actually get close enough to him to kiss him. Just standing there with him was enough for the pure, potent sensuality he exuded to seep into her pores and turn on things inside her that shouldn't be turned on.

"This is crazy," she murmured.

"Runs in the family," he confided. "I can't let you go without gettin' at least what you gave Buzz or he'll never let me hear the end of it." Shane raised his chin and his voice, aiming both in the direction from which they'd just come. "Isn't that right, Buzz? You're in there listenin' to all this, aren't you?"

"She's not gonna do it. It's me she's partial to," the old man called back.

Maya couldn't help laughing at the two of them.

"I'm not lettin' her go till she does," Shane insisted, meaning it for both Buzz and Maya.

"I don't believe this," she said.

Shane leaned down so he was closer to her height,

closed his eyes and poked his cheek once again. "Believe it."

"Aw, go ahead and give 'im a little smooch, Maya. Make the boy's day," Buzz urged from the bedroom.

She didn't know how long these two rascals would keep this up or how long Shane might be willing to detain her. But she decided it was probably easier and quicker to comply than to fight it. Besides, she didn't want to seem like a spoilsport since she knew they were only teasing her.

And if a tiny part of her might have been urging her to do it for her own sake, she tried not to admit it to herself.

She sighed loudly, rose up on tiptoe and jabbed a quick kiss on Shane's cheek to match the one she'd given his grandfather.

That's all there was to it, and as soon as she'd done it, Shane stood straight again, opened his eyes and smiled down at her as he called to Buzz, "Got one."

"Pretty nice, wasn't it?"

"Pretty nice," Shane agreed in a softer tone that seemed for Maya's ears alone.

She just rolled her eyes and shook her head, hoping it hid the fact that the simple buss had rocked her. The scent of Shane's aftershave still filled her nostrils. The warm, rough texture of his whisker-roughened skin seemed to have imprinted itself on her lips. And she had a terrible urge to kiss more than his cheek....

"I have to go," she said suddenly, more insistently than she had before.

"But you'll be back," he said, sounding thrilled by the prospect.

"Sometime," was all she would promise as she hurried outside and took a deep breath of country air, hoping it would clear her head.

But what it didn't do was take away the impact of having been so near to Shane McDermot. Or the desire to be there again.

"Well, that was a first," she muttered as she got into her mother's car.

She'd never had to kiss her way out of a house before. And in reality, she could have refused to this time. She could have sternly put Shane McDermot in his place. She could have told him in no uncertain terms that she was there to do a job and nothing more, and that she wouldn't stand for foolishness like that.

She could have.

She probably should have.

But she hadn't.

Instead she'd gone along with it.

She'd actually *kissed* him, she thought now, amazed at herself and finding it harder and harder to fathom as she drove away from the house.

But she'd done it all right. She'd kissed Shane McDermot.

Kissed him and liked it, heaven help her.

Kissed him, liked it and come away torn between being annoyed with herself for letting such an unprofessional thing happen…and fostering a secret thrill that it had.

Three

"I still can't believe you're Elk Creek's nurse—"

"And physical therapist and midwife."

"And physical therapist and midwife," Maya echoed, marveling for the second time late the next afternoon that the woman providing Buzz Martindale's medical care was the third member—along with Maya and Kansas—of the inseparable threesome she'd been part of growing up.

Margie had remembered only that morning to tell Maya that Tallie Shanahan was back and wearing many medical hats for the small town. Maya couldn't have been more surprised, since she hadn't had so much as a card from Tallie in eight years.

"*I* still can't believe you're the caseworker who's checking on old Buzz," Tallie countered as they settled in Tallie's office in the medical facility that acted as doctor's office, dentist's office, outpatient surgery center and makeshift temporary hospital when necessary.

"Small world," Tallie added. "Or do all roads lead home to Elk Creek?"

"I'm just here on a working visit," Maya was quick

to say, lest her friend get the mistaken idea she'd moved back permanently.

"Maybe it'll grow on you again. I know it's grown on me and I've only been here two weeks."

"It isn't the town," Maya said. "I've always liked Elk Creek. It's some of the people in it who I'd rather not be anywhere near. So tell me about yourself—are you attached? Unattached?"

"Un. How about you?"

"I'm unattached, too." But the oddest thing happened to Maya as she said that. The image of Shane McDermot popped into her mind. Of course, it had been popping in—and lingering—with persistent regularity since leaving him the day before. But his image popping into her head when she was talking about whether or not there was a man in her life compounded the oddity.

"We'll have to get together with Kansas—just the three of us, like old times—and catch up on everything," Tallie suggested.

"I'm game if we do it with only the three of us."

Tallie's well-shaped eyebrows edged toward her hairline. "You don't sound too eager. Has something happened between you and Kansas that I don't know about?"

"No. I'd just rather not run into her husband."

"Linc Heller," Tallie said, as if light had dawned. "I'd forgotten about how you feel about the Hellers and all that. Guess it's been a long time."

Not long enough for Maya to forget, but she didn't

say that. She didn't have to say anything as Tallie went on.

"I always thought it would work out for your mom with Shag Heller. Or maybe I just hoped it would so Suzy Teeblat and her crew could eat their words."

Instead Margie had been terribly hurt and Suzy Teeblat and her crew had had the opportunity to rub salt in those wounds.

But Maya didn't want to talk about that. "Like you said, it was a long time ago."

"But you still feel awkward around the Hellers."

She did. Not that it had been the Hellers who were her peers who had made her miserable as a teenager. The nastiness had all come from people who weren't even friends of theirs. But still, things between Maya and Shag Heller's offspring had been uncomfortable, and she had no more desire to have close contact with any of them now than she'd had years ago.

Maya shrugged. "I'd just like to keep any getting together we might do with Kansas somewhere her husband isn't likely to be."

"Easy enough."

"Now tell me about Buzz," Maya said to get off the other subject altogether.

Tallie didn't seem to have a problem turning to business. She gave Maya a complete history and update on the elderly gentleman, who apparently had lost as much of his will to take care of himself as he had his capacity since the death of his wife.

"But he's perked right up being here," Tallie said.

"From what I can see, it's done a world of good for him."

"And what about the family?" Maya asked. It was a question she routinely posed in this situation. But now it had a personal resonance to it and she knew it was only because of Shane and the strange fact that she couldn't quite disconnect from him for some reason.

"The family seems to be doing well, too," Tallie said. "From what I've seen in just a short time, anyway. Ry is great. He's patient with the old man. He makes sure everything is being taken care of if he doesn't do it himself. And he seems to be genuinely happy to have Buzz in the house."

"Ry. That's Shane's brother, right? What about Shane?"

Tallie's pretty pink mouth eased into what looked like an embarrassed smile. "The same was true of Shane, too, for the three days he was there with Buzz before he had to go on that trip he just made. I was only mentioning Ry because he's been around and I sort of forgot about Shane."

Forgot about him? How was that possible? Unless the reason Tallie was embarrassed had less to do with leaving out Shane than it did with having her focus so concentrated on his brother.

"Is something going on between you and Ry?"

"No! Why would you think that?"

The answer seemed too quick and made Maya smile

at her old friend. "Are you a little taken with Ry McDermot?"

"Who, me? No. I mean, he's nice. And good-looking and...all. But I've barely spoken to him three or four times and only about Buzz. Most of what I know about his response to his grandfather is what Junebug and Buzz himself have told me."

"This is me you're talking to, Tallie. Remember? We had our first crush together. On the same boy."

"Cully Culhane," Tallie said with a warm laugh Maya realized she had missed all these years.

"And now it's Ry McDermot."

"You have a crush on Ry?" Tallie asked, misunderstanding.

"No, I don't. I haven't even met him yet. But I think you do."

"Don't be silly. I don't. I just admire the way he's treating Buzz."

Tallie said that so sincerely Maya wondered if maybe she had read too much into her friend's words and expression. Maybe she had projected her own inability to stop thinking about Shane onto Tallie.

Or perhaps Tallie was just having the same problem with Ry haunting her thoughts that Maya was having with Shane haunting hers. And if so, maybe it didn't mean any more to Tallie than it did to Maya. Maybe it was only a strange nuisance to her, too.

Nothing worth discussing. So Maya just let that subject drop, too.

"Well, shall we go out to the ranch, then? I'd like to see how Buzz is doing with therapy."

"You picked a good day. I finally got the walker I ordered for him and I'm going to teach him how to use it," Tallie said enthusiastically.

But somehow Maya had the feeling all that enthusiasm wasn't centered on getting old Buzz to take his first few steps. She thought it had more to do with the chance that Tallie would get to see Ry McDermot.

Or maybe Maya was just projecting her own feelings once again. Because the truth was, she was itching to get out to that ranch herself. And what was causing that itching was the thought that she might encounter Shane once she got there....

"Don't bother. If I couldn't get that female grizzly bear to let me in dressed like this, you two are never going to set eyes on him."

Maya and Tallie had driven out to the McDermot ranch in separate cars in case either of them finished their business before the other and wanted to leave. But they'd arrived at the same time, parked in tandem behind a battered old convertible in front of the house and headed up the tiled walkway together.

As they did, a bosomy woman with bottle red hair a mile high, wearing a skin-tight leotard with stiletto heels and sporting enough jewelry to be a metal detector's worst nightmare, stopped pounding on the door and came in their direction like a bull for a matador's cape.

Maya glanced down at her own conservative khaki slacks and white oxford shirt, and then at Tallie's all-white nurse's uniform, and decided they weren't the ones with anything to be ashamed of.

"Besides," the other woman said in a bitchy voice with a nod at the walker Tallie was carrying with her, "I can tell you both that you're not Shane McDermot's type whether those getups are for real or you're offering something kinky. So give up and pack it in."

Maya and Tallie merely smiled politely and went around the woman.

Not until they were out of her hearing range did Tallie whisper, "Guess she thinks I came to play doctor."

"Yeah, but what's kinky about me?" Maya whispered back with a laugh.

They rang the doorbell and moments later heard from inside, "This better not be one o' you hot-to-trot she-wolves, or so help me, I'm gonna come after you with a cattle prod."

Tallie chuckled and confided to Maya, "Ever since that article in *Prominence Magazine* named Shane as one of the world's most eligible bachelors, women have been crawling all over Elk Creek and the ranch looking for him. One of them even broke into the house and got into bed with Buzz last week, thinking it might be Shane's bed." Then, calling back through the panel, she said, "It's just me, Junebug. And Maya Wilson."

"Praise the Lord and be thankful. I can't take no more o' those other kind today," the voice muttered as the door finally opened.

And there stood Junebug Brimley, all six feet, three hundred pounds of her, dressed in a loud Hawaiian-print shirt over yellow stretch pants, her white hair pulled into a sugar-doughnut-size bun on top of her head and her meaty face a road map of lines.

Her small brown eyes honed in on Maya and took root.

"Is that really you, Maya honey? Margie's baby girl?" she asked in a voice as sweet as honey.

"It's me," Maya confirmed, and was embraced in a hug that could have come from a grizzly bear.

"Hi there to you, too, Tallie," Junebug added as she released Maya. "I knew you were comin' today but I didn't know 'bout Maya here. It's so good to see you. Your mama don't complain but you don't come home near often enough."

"It's good to see you, too, Junebug."

"Did you both come to deal with that old stinker laid up in the bedroom or can we visit in the kitchen a little?"

"Actually, I'd like to talk to you," Maya answered.

"I can't do much visiting today," Tallie put in. "Buzz and I have some work to do with this walker. We'll get him used to it so he can start doing a few things for himself."

"Hallelujah!" Junebug said with her eyes raised heavenward. "Go to it, then, child. I'm all for anythin' that gets that crotchety old buzzard outta my hair some," she added without malice so Maya knew she didn't mean it.

"See you all later," Tallie said, taking the walker with her down the hall to Buzz's bedroom.

"Come on with me," Junebug said, wasting no time in crossing the foyer to the great room, barreling through it to the enormous formal dining room that lay beyond it and going into the kitchen from there, all with Maya having to increase her pace considerably to keep up.

"How's your mama?" Junebug asked on the way.

"Same as always. Good."

"And what about you? I hear you're the social worker come to look in on old Buzz."

"You heard right."

At one end of the kitchen was a U-shaped breakfast nook that took up the full wall and at least six feet of both side walls. Maya guessed it would seat more than a dozen people comfortably as Junebug motioned for her to slide in and brought to the table a colander full of fresh fruit, which she began slicing into a bowl.

After inquiring about Junebug's husband and six grown sons, Maya slipped casually into work and began to question her about Buzz.

It wasn't a subject that was hard to get Junebug to warm up to. She took care of Buzz along with the house and cooking through the day, so she knew what was going on, and she had an opinion on just about everything.

Maya listened carefully, but her eyes tended to drift even as she did. The kitchen seemed to be the heart of the house, connecting all portions of it by a number of doors. She couldn't help casting a glance toward the door she and Junebug had come through from the dining room and the doors she assumed led to the bedroom wings. Then she glanced out the wall of French doors to the patio and what stretched into barnyard beyond it.

But it wasn't with Buzz in mind that she scanned her surroundings.

It was Shane who once more kept emerging in her thoughts as she wondered where he was or if he might come in through one of those doors sometime soon.

Not that she had any idea if there was a chance of that or if he was even home today. And not that she cared, she told herself. She was just curious.

Junebug was in the middle of telling her that someone ought to force Buzz to eat the broccoli she had planned for dinner, when Maya thought she saw Shane come out of a barn that looked brand-spanking new.

She didn't want to perk up at the sight of him, but she suddenly found herself sitting straighter and taller on the breakfast nook's bench seat, even craning her head somewhat.

But was it Shane or wasn't it?

The man who came out of the barn had on a gray T-shirt and leather chaps over blue jeans, and for all intents and purposes, he looked like Shane. But there was something about him that made Maya think it wasn't Shane.

Nothing concrete. The man was the same height. The same build. He had the same hair. The same face.

But as she watched him stop to talk to a ranch hand, Maya didn't feel anything. No stirring. No weak knees or breathlessness or craving to be with him. Nothing but an objective acknowledgment that he was a terrific-looking guy.

Maybe it was Shane and she'd finally gained that immunity she'd been hoping—and trying—for, she told herself, thinking what a relief it would be if that was true.

But then Junebug apparently noticed that she was staring out at the man and dashed her hopes. "That's Ry," Junebug informed her.

Ry. Shane's twin. Not Shane himself.

Did that mean Ry didn't affect her the way Shane did? Or had she really gained that immunity regardless of which of the McDermot twins she spotted?

She was keeping her fingers crossed.

"They do look alike," Maya commented.

"Spittin' image of each other. I can't hardly tell 'em apart, 'cept for Shane's got a scar in his eyebrow. That's what I look for. That and what clothes they have on when I see 'em in the mornin'."

"I noticed the scar," Maya said. And she was dying to ask how he got it but was afraid of showing too much interest and turning into a woman like those who were chasing after him.

Then she was saved from her own curiosity by the appearance of Tallie in the doorway Maya had assumed led from the bedroom wing.

"Well, we've achieved mobility," Tallie announced.

"Hallelujah!" Junebug repeated.

"I want Buzz to take it slow. I don't want him to go on any long treks, nothing outside the house for now. But he can make it to the dinner table tonight. You won't need to be serving him his meals in bed anymore."

"Did you talk to him about eating his broccoli?"

Obviously this was one of the ongoing arguments between Junebug and Buzz.

"I told him it was good for him," Tallie conceded. "But I don't think it made any difference."

"Stubborn old mule."

"I need to be going now," Tallie said as if to escape being in the middle of the dispute. "The Ladies Club meeting is at my house tonight and we're having a birthday dinner for one of the members." Then to Maya, she said, "Is your mom coming or is she passing on it to stay with you? Not that you aren't welcome, too, because you are."

"Mom is going but I'm not. Thanks, anyway."

"I hate to take her away when you're home visiting."

"It's all right. I wouldn't want her to miss anything she had planned on my account."

"Think it over. If you change your mind, I'll see

you later. Otherwise, I'll probably see you over here or I'll call to set up a time to get together,'' Tallie said.

Goodbyes made their rounds, and once Tallie had gone, Maya slid out of the nook.

"Well, I think I'll look in on Buzz and stop distracting you from your cooking."

"You aren't distractin' me. I'm happy for the company. But if I keep you to myself much longer, pretty soon he'll be feelin' sorry for himself,'' Junebug agreed. Then she pointed to the door Tallie had just come through. "Easiest way to get to his room from here is through there—follow the hall to the last door on the left goin' from that direction. And don't forget about that broccoli."

Maya just laughed, said, "Thanks," and left the kitchen.

Buzz's bedroom door was open when she got there so she knocked on the jamb.

"I'm in here," he called from the sitting room.

Maya went through the bedroom to the connecting door and came upon the old man as he maneuvered the walker across the plush white shag carpet, favoring his hurt leg with only scant weight put on it. He was dressed in those same disreputable cowboy boots and soiled hat, this time wearing a green terry-cloth bathrobe over his underclothes.

"You're looking pretty spry," Maya said as she went far enough into the room to stand behind an easy chair and watch him make slow progress to the sofa that faced it.

"Spry 'nuff to chase you around if you give me half a chance," he answered even as he plopped down on the couch. "Ah, now that feels good. Sittin' on real furniture 'stead of bein' in that dad-blamed bed. Thought I might die in it."

"Tallie says you're doing well."

"Hell, yes, I am. I'll be out on the range 'fore long to see what those boys've done to the place."

"We've let it all go to pot—what do you think we've done to it?" Shane's rich, deep voice came from the connecting doorway behind Maya and washed over her like warm honey.

So much for having achieved immunity to him.

She did a half turn to look at him and found the big, tall, work-dirty cowboy standing there holding soiled leather gloves in one hand and a sweat-stained hat in the other. He had on blue jeans that were grimy and a red western shirt with circles under each arm. His face was shadowed with a day's growth of beard, and he smelled of horse.

Maya couldn't help thinking, If only all the women who were after him could see him now....

But even if they could, they'd probably have the same reaction she was having. In spite of the way he looked—and smelled—she felt her pulse kick up a notch and send out a rush of pure joy at that first sight of him, proving that he was definitely one of the world's most appealing men.

To her, anyway. No matter how much she wished it wasn't so.

He winked at her in greeting, smiled a smile that could curl her toes all by itself and said, "Are we talkin' broccoli in here?"

He must have come through the kitchen a split second after she'd left it, Maya thought.

"Not yet," she answered.

"Old woman," Buzz muttered. "I'm not eatin' that green poison and she might as well quit naggin' at me 'bout it. And don't neither of you say how good fer me it is. I don't give a diddly damn whether it'll make me git up and dance a jig after one bite. I'm not eatin' it and that's that."

"Would it help if we could persuade Maya to stay for supper? Would you eat it then?" Shane proposed with a note of teasing in his voice.

"We already went through this yesterday," she pointed out.

"Nothin' says you can't stay and have a meal with friends when the clock stops, does it?" Shane countered. "It doesn't have to have anything to do with work. And Junebug already told me you'd be eatin' by your lonesome if you don't stay."

Interesting that that was the one piece of information Junebug had chosen to relay as Shane passed through the kitchen.

"Eatin' by yerself?" Buzz chimed in as if it were a crime in the making. "We ain't gonna have that!"

"It'd be unneighborly," Shane added. Then he

dipped his chin and said in a more confidential tone, "Besides, I just got here and haven't had the chance to even say hello. You can't go runnin' off now."

"Hey, Junebug!" Buzz bellowed. "Set a place for little Maya. She's stayin' fer supper to celebrate my gittin' to eat at the table tonight."

Maya knew she should put up a strong protest. She knew she should flat out refuse to stay. She knew she should cut short any time she had with Shane or she would never gain any immunity to his appeal.

But that appeal was stronger than she was. Especially when leaving at that moment would mean having spent only those few minutes with him.

"Junebug doesn't need another mouth to feed," she said in a feeble attempt to salvage her pride and not seem like just another woman in pursuit of Shane. Which she wasn't, she told herself defensively.

"Junebug always cooks enough for an army," Shane assured her. "And if it'll make you feel any better, you can help me wash dishes afterward—it's my night for it."

"You expect me to believe you wash dishes?" she said dubiously. After all, the man was worth a fortune and rich men didn't do their own dishes. Did they?

"Well, I don't actually wash them. But it's my night to clear the table and put them in the dishwasher. We can't have Junebug makin' her own family wait any longer than they already do for their supper just so she can clean our mess."

Maya doubted any of the women who were after

him envisioned him as he was now—sweaty, grimy and whiskered after a day's work—let alone doing dishes on top of it.

"Come on, little Maya. Say you'll stay," Buzz cajoled.

She shook her head like a mother indulging two children, when, in fact, it was herself she was indulging. "Okay. Since I've had my arm just about twisted off."

Shane grinned at her and slapped the leather gloves against his thigh, sending up a puff of dust. "Great! Just let me take a quick shower and we'll get to it."

Maya's gaze involuntarily followed him out of the room and as far down the hall as was possible without being obvious. Then, hoping the older man hadn't noticed, she accepted Buzz's invitation to sit a spell.

She didn't yet consider herself off the clock—as Shane had put it—so she settled in to question the elderly man more extensively about his health and happiness.

His outlook seemed good, and the one thing that was evident in everything he said was how glad and grateful he was to have his family around him. Try as she might, she could find no fault in the current living arrangement, except maybe that it hadn't begun before Buzz got hurt.

"Okay, you old bear, let's see what you can do with that walker," was how Shane announced his return forty-five minutes later and the fact that it was time to go in to dinner.

He crossed to his grandfather in long strides and held the metal contraption for Buzz. While Buzz got to his feet, Maya stood, too, taking in the sight of Shane as she did.

His shower had brought about an improvement. His hair was shiny clean, and he was freshly shaven and smelled like heaven instead of horses. He wore a crisp white shirt with a red-and-gray pattern in the tips of the pointed western yolk, and a pair of silver gray twill jeans that hugged his hips and derriere so smoothly they might have been specially tailored for him. In fact, they fitted him so well it was difficult for Maya to unglue her gaze from his back pockets, and only when he stepped out of his grandfather's way and robbed her of the view did she manage to extract her attention from the admiration of hind parts she had no business admiring.

Buzz led them out of the room and down the hall at a snail's pace, with Shane staying patiently nearby and holding out an arm to catch the older man if he fell.

Maya was glad to see it. It went a long way in showing her the care and compassion Shane felt for his grandfather.

The table had been set in the breakfast nook in the kitchen, surprising Maya slightly. She'd half expected the formal dining room to be used and realized that she'd unconsciously been thinking of Shane as a rich rancher who wouldn't dirty his hands as he had today or take his meals in the kitchen. Let alone clean up after himself.

But the kitchen it was, as Junebug set out roast beef, mashed potatoes, a green salad and the controversial broccoli.

Shane helped Buzz ease into one end of the bench seat and brought him a stool to keep his leg elevated. Then he motioned Maya to slide around to the back of the table and shouted, "Soup's on, Ry."

Maya laughed to herself at the further evidence of just how down-home the man was.

"That's it for me, folks," Junebug said as she set the bowl of fruit she'd sliced earlier on the countertop, apparently for dessert. "Like I tell you every night, you can leave them dishes for me to do in the morning if you want, but I'm bound for home now."

"Have a nice night, Junebug," Shane said.

"You, too," Junebug answered with a chuckle and a knowing note in her voice.

She headed for the door to the dining room, hitting it just as the man Maya had seen in the barnyard came through from the other direction. He stopped short and held the swinging door wide for her while Maya called goodbye and Buzz muttered, "Hope you're plannin' on eatin' broccoli fer yer lunch tomorrow."

Junebug pretended not to hear the comment, said good-night to Ry and left.

Then in came Ry.

Shane introduced him to Maya, and no sooner was he finished than Buzz said, "These two is twins."

Ry laughed warmly and shook his head at Maya.
"Bet you never would have guessed that."

"Shane's the oldest by five minutes and the more
outgoin' of the two of 'em," Buzz continued, his pride
in his grandsons echoing in his tone. "But one's as
good a man as the other and they're both better'n any
I've ever known."

Shane looked at Ry. "He's gonna have me blushin'
in a minute. How 'bout you?"

"Nah. It's the truth," Ry joked back.

And so started a lively dinner that put Maya at ease
with the three men as they kept conversation going
with little effort on her part.

It left her able to study the two brothers without
seeming to. And study them she did.

The resemblance between them was uncanny. There
were only minor differences she could discern as she
glanced surreptitiously from one handsome face to the
other. Differences that would be hard to spot unless
the two men were sitting side by side and only a few
feet away as they were through that meal.

Ry's nose was a mere millimeter longer than
Shane's and his hair had the faintest touch of sun
streaks that were a shade lighter. Shane's bottom lip
was minutely fuller than his brother's and his chin a
tad more pronounced.

But Junebug had been right, the only real way to
tell them apart if they weren't shoulder to shoulder
was the slight jag Shane's left eyebrow took where
that almost invisible scar creased it.

Well, maybe that wasn't the *only* way, Maya realized as the meal wore on. Because her response to the two men seemed to be a pretty reliable gauge, too.

What had happened earlier, when she'd first spied Ry outside, held true as she sat around the corner of the table from them. When Ry talked to her, his voice didn't feel as if it were doing a feather dance along her nerve endings the way Shane's every word did. When Ry looked at her, no liquid warmth ran through her veins the way it did with one glance from those green eyes of Shane's. When Ry smiled at her, it didn't send goose bumps up her arms or make her insides melt—both things that Shane could elicit with the slightest curve of the corners of his mouth.

And by the time they reached dessert, it wasn't Ry she began to think about being alone with. It was Shane.

She didn't understand it. Didn't understand how she could be so overwhelmingly drawn to him and not to a man who looked exactly like him. A man who was every bit as nice, as personable, as charming.

But that was how it was.

Which made the intensity of her attraction to Shane all the more disconcerting, because if there was no reason or rationale to it, how was she ever going to resist his allure?

By the time the meal was finished, Buzz was visibly tiring and both grandsons seemed tuned in to it. After reminding Shane that it was his night for dishes, Ry urged the elderly man back into the walker with the bribe of a rodeo playing on television and the promise that he'd stay in Buzz's room to watch it with him.

Buzz paused once he was in the walker and confided to Maya, "They're coddlin' me to death. Just wait'll I get their tails out on the range and ride rings 'round 'em. They'll be beggin' me to have mercy 'stead of treatin' me like some young pup," he said as if he were thoroughly enjoying the attention in spite of the complaint. Then he kissed his fingertips and tossed the kiss to her. "'Night, little Maya," he added with a wink that had probably won him a lot of female hearts in his day and showed her where his grandsons had inherited some of their rakish appeal.

"Good night, Buzz. Thanks for dinner. I enjoyed myself."

"Anytime, sweetheart. Anytime."

"Nice meetin' you, Maya," Ry said as he followed the old man out of the kitchen.

"You, too," Maya called after them.

And then she was alone with Shane.

He'd spent a fair amount of the meal watching her. She'd caught him at it several times and felt it the rest. But now he was staring openly. And smiling a Cheshire cat smile that made her feel like something he was pleased to have spotted under a microscope.

"Better get to these dishes," she said to divert his interest.

It didn't. He just went on studying her.

"I was only teasin' about you havin' to help with

that,'' he said in a voice more intimate than he'd used all evening.

''But I want to,'' she insisted, stacking plates to busy herself.

Something about that made him chuckle to himself—a sound that rumbled deep in his chest—and she sensed that he knew she was as antsy as a wallflower being asked to dance by the homecoming king.

Then he seemed to take pity on her and he grabbed two serving dishes, taking them with him as he slid out of the nook.

''We only do a makeshift job of it. We just cover the food and stick it in the fridge for Junebug to do whatever she's gonna do with it later, rinse the plates and stick them in the dishwasher, wipe off the table and things,'' he explained.

Movement and not being under his scrutiny put her more at ease and made her bold enough to ask a question she'd been wondering about since he'd told her it was his night for kitchen cleanup. ''So what kind of living in the lap of luxury is it when you do your own dishes?''

His brows pulled together in a fleeting frown. ''Who said anything about livin' in the lap of luxury?''

Maya shot a glance around the room. ''This place isn't exactly a hovel. And from the stuff that's been written about you—''

''Most of that's hogwash.''

''Okay. But I would think you'd have someone

other than just Junebug to take care of things around here.''

He took an exaggerated look at the paper-thin watch that wrapped his wrist. ''Are we back on the clock now and you're tellin' me I should have more than Junebug around for Buzz's sake?''

''No,'' she said quickly. ''I'm not on the clock and that's not what I'm saying. I'm just trying to figure you out.''

He seemed to like that, because a sexy smile returned to his lips. ''That so? How come?'' he added with a wicked arch to that one quirky eyebrow.

''I'm just curious. Junebug does a fine job, and from what I've seen so far, Buzz is being well taken care of. I was only wondering.''

His supple mouth stretched into a grin as he took the last of the plates she'd brought from the table. ''I don't want to get spoiled,'' he said, as if he were kidding.

''Spoiled?'' She reached for a sponge and pointed with it to the rest of the room. ''I think it's too late.''

''Livin' in this place is one thing. It's comfortable and it serves its purpose. But a lot of the other perks money can buy can change a person. Make them forget where they came from. Who they really are. What's important. Doin' dishes, ridin' a train keeps you knowin' what you're about.''

''And what are you about?'' she asked, feeling a serious urge to know.

''Guess I'm about muckin' around in the dirt and

dung, and breakin' horses, and herdin' cattle, and ridin' trains and doin' dishes.''

"And taking care of your grandfather."

"That, too."

"You don't seem to mind."

"Why would I mind? I hated it when he and my grandmother moved away from here. I didn't get to know them till late. I missed out on all but a couple years with my grandmother, but I don't want to miss out on any time I might have left with old Buzz."

"How did that come about, anyway—your family getting back together after all those years not speaking?'' she ventured, since he'd made reference to the rift.

"Times change people. Mature them, if they're lucky. Sometimes it gives them an example to show them someone else's point of view. For my mother it was my sister, Kate.''

"You have a sister?''

"Just one. And Ry and two other brothers, too.''

"But it was your sister who showed your mother another point of view?''

"Yep. She turned seventeen.''

"That's all it took?''

"Seventeen is when my mother dropped out of high school to run off and marry my father. It's when old Buzz hit the ceiling, all hell broke loose and they stopped havin' anything to do with each other.''

"I can't say I blame him for being upset about a seventeen-year-old dropping out of school and marrying. In my job I come across too many tragedies that have beginnings like that.''

''My mother couldn't blame him, either, when my sister put her in Buzz's shoes. Kate fancied herself in love and started talkin' about doin' the same thing Mom and Dad did.''

''Ah…''

''It didn't seem nearly so romantic when my mother was the parent. Even though my folks've been happy together all this time, they still didn't want Kate doin' it. And that made them both start to think that Buzz hadn't been so out of line.''

''And what about Buzz? Was he receptive to a reunion?''

''Wasn't Buzz my mother called the first time. It was my grandmother. But time had softened things here, too. Buzz saw that the marriage had worked out and he wanted to meet his grandchildren. What had separated them before wasn't so important anymore.''

''So everything worked out all right.''

It was Shane's turn to glance around the room and chuckle again. ''Looks like it.''

''Where are your folks now?''

''In Texas still. So are my other two brothers and Kate. But the folks are sellin' the spread there and it looks like Kate and the boys might end up here, too.''

''Are you okay with that?''

''Sure. It's as much theirs as Ry's and mine. Buzz put the original ranch in all five of our names when he couldn't work it anymore, but my dad needed at least two of us to run the Texas property with him. Ry and I had some plans of our own—we wanted to try a new breed of cattle, do some experimentin'—so we came up here. But when we built the house, we did it with the idea of everybody livin' in Elk Creek if they wanted to.''

Shane closed the dishwasher, took the sponge Maya had used to wipe off the table and countertops as they'd talked and put it away.

''So here we are—the McDermots and the Martindales one big happy family again, and you and I done with the dishes.''

Maya was surprised to find he was right about the dishes. The time had gone so quickly she hadn't realized they'd completely spruced up the kitchen. But they had, and it left her with no legitimate reason for continuing the evening. Like it or not.

''I think I better call it a night,'' she forced herself to say. And it did take a force of will when every moment she was with Shane she liked him more and more.

''I thought I might be able to talk you into a nightcap. Maybe out on the patio since the weather's nice. Under the stars. Or in the den—you still haven't seen the den. Or we could have a game of pool? You haven't seen the rec room yet, either.''

It was flattering to know he wasn't eager to draw a close to the evening himself. And it was tempting—very tempting—to take him up on any one of his suggestions. Especially when she imagined herself and

Shane outside on the patio. Wine in hand. Breathing in the perfume of clear country air. Alone in the quiet of the spring night…

But into that fantasy came her mother's voice telling her it was better to be a rich man's treasure, which was what Margie had thought herself to be at one time.

And it threw a bucket of cold water onto Maya's musings. "No, thanks. I need to get back," she said firmly.

"You say that like you think I'm gonna turn into a werewolf soon as the moon gets high."

In a way that wasn't too far from just what she thought, if not literally, then at least figuratively.

"I promise I won't, if that helps any," he added with a tone in his voice and an expression on his handsome face that were so inviting they made her resolve waver.

But only slightly. "I really can't stay."

"You're gonna go off and leave me lonely?" he teased.

"You don't have to be lonely and we both know it. All you have to do is whistle and some woman or another will come out of the woodwork to keep you company."

"Is that so?"

"Tallie told me one of them even broke into your house last week. And I saw for myself what happened on the train. Plus, Junebug was chasing off someone when Tallie and I got here today."

He made a great show of looking beyond her,

through the floor-to-ceiling wall of glass that framed the patio that had been the backdrop for her fantasy.

"I don't see anybody climbin' in the window or flashin' me or needin' to be chased off now," he pointed out.

"Just wait awhile," she advised. "I'm sure someone to your liking will come along."

He was leaning with his hips against the sink, his legs stretched out and crossed at the ankles and his arms folded over his chest. His eyes were focused intently on her. "Could be someone to my liking already has come along. But she's harder than a jackrabbit to pin down."

Okay, so the man had more than his fair share of charisma, and rather than gaining immunity to it, she seemed to be getting more susceptible. But thoughts of all the women he could pick and choose from helped shore her defenses.

"I really have to go," she repeated.

He took a deep breath and sighed it out, making his chest rise and fall in a fantastic swell that her gaze rode hungrily along on. But he finally conceded, "Guess it wouldn't do to hog-tie the caseworker to keep her here. Probably reflect badly in her report."

"Probably would."

"Then let me at least walk you out to your car."

"That you can do," she agreed, only because now that the moment of actually leaving had been accomplished, some contrary part of her didn't want to go.

Didn't want to end this time with him, and having him see her out extended it, if only by a few minutes.

Shane pushed off the counter's edge with another sigh and preceded her to the door to hold it open for her. She went through in front of him, trying not to be so aware of his potent masculinity as she maneuvered around his big, solidly packed man's body.

She could hear the television on in Buzz's room as they made their way across the dining room and then the great room to the foyer, could hear Buzz's voice raised in a hoot over something he was watching.

She decided not to interrupt by calling goodbye and merely let Shane open the front door for her so she could step out into the cool May evening air.

And the first thing she thought when it brushed her skin was that it would have been a beautiful evening for sipping a nightcap on the patio. But it was too late for that, and she was better off going home, anyway, she told herself, trying to believe it.

Shane held the driver's side door to her mother's car open for her, as well, closing it after her once she'd gotten in. But he didn't merely say good-night from there. Instead he laid a hand on the roof and leaned into the open window so that he was near enough for her to smell the lingering scent of his aftershave. So that, if things were different, she might have thought he was going to kiss her.

Which, of course, was silly.

Wasn't it?

"Well, good night," she said in a hurry, trying to outrun her own thoughts.

"I'm glad you stayed for supper," he said with an echo of laughter in his voice, as if he knew what she was thinking and how it unnerved her again.

"Me, too. Thanks," she blurted out as she turned the key in the ignition, hoping for a quick getaway.

But the car didn't start. It made a feeble growling noise and stopped. She tried again and it did the same thing.

Don't do this to me, she silently beseeched the vehicle, trying a third time with no more luck.

"I think she's dead," Shane observed.

Still Maya made a fourth and a fifth attempt, but to no avail.

"Damn," she muttered under her breath.

"Looks like you'll have to stay the night," Shane teased with lascivious delight.

"I don't think so," Maya said, but the engine still didn't turn over on the sixth try.

"Shame," he muttered, but she wasn't sure whether he thought it was a shame that the car wouldn't start or that she wouldn't spend the night. Then he said, "S'pose I'll have to give you a ride home if you're dead set against a sleepover."

She turned the key once more but it didn't matter and she finally had to accept that the car just wasn't going to give her a break and start.

This time it was Maya who sighed, only her sigh had a tinge of frustration in it.

"I'm definitely dead set against a sleepover, but it looks like I'm going to need that ride home."

With her final concession, he straightened up and opened the door again. Before she could get out, he offered her a helping hand.

It seemed rude not to take it, even as an instant war raged inside her between the faction that wanted to and the one that was worried what physical contact with him might do to her when simple glances or the sound of his voice had such impact.

But manners and the faction in favor won the battle, and she took the hand he offered.

That's when she knew she was in serious trouble. Her hand slipped into his as if it had been cut from it. And when he closed those long, thick fingers around it, when the warmth of his skin engulfed hers, when the feel of toughened calluses titillated her, it was as if something more than his hand had reached out and grabbed hold of her. As if a much more important, inexplicable—almost enchanted—connection had been made.

But maybe it was all in her mind, because Shane didn't seem affected by it. He just held her hand until she'd gotten out of the car and then let go of it as he nodded in the direction of the tan-colored truck parked not far away.

"Come on, let's take Ry's wheels. Keys are probably in it."

Maya didn't say anything. She just went along beside him, climbing into the passenger seat with that same hand of Shane's at her back as she did.

She couldn't say anything. She was too dumb-founded by what had just happened to her, too lost in thought about whether or not she'd imagined it. Whether or not she was the only one of them to feel it.

Shane didn't say much, either, on the drive to her mother's house just off Center Street. It seemed strange, because he was usually so talkative. But that didn't necessarily mean he'd been rocked by whatever it was she'd felt happen between them moments earlier.

He stopped the truck in front of her mother's house and got out, coming around to Maya's side. He opened the door yet again and held out his hand for her.

She was almost afraid to take it. But afraid or not, she was drawn to it like a moth to a flame.

And yes, she felt that same intense, instinctual connection just the way she had before.

I've gone insane, she thought as she stepped out of the truck.

Only Shane didn't let go of her hand this time. He hung on to it all the way up the walk to the front porch.

Say something, she ordered herself, trying to regain any amount of control.

"I'll have to get a mechanic to meet me at your place tomorrow to fix the car," she finally managed.

"Mmm," was all he said as they stepped into the

pale glow of the porch light that her mother had left on.

"Thanks for the lift home."

"Sure," he said in a quiet, almost ruminative voice as he faced her.

He caught her eyes with his and looked so intently into them that it crossed her mind that he was searching for something. But she didn't know what. Unless it was for a sign of the effect he'd had on her by just holding her hand.

And he was still holding it. Caressing it now with light strokes of his thumb that set off glittering sparks from that spot all the way up her arm.

Then he kissed her.

She didn't see it coming. But she was so lost in what his touch could do to her that even if there had been signs of it, she knew she would have missed them. She almost missed the kiss itself because it was so quick, so brief. Really just a scant brushing of his lips against hers.

Yet it was enough to go straight to her head. To make her lean slightly forward, as if he might do it again. Wishing he would...

He didn't, though. Instead he let her go, whispered a soft, "'Night," and left as if someone were chasing him away.

And as she watched him go, she warned herself again that she was on dangerous territory with him.

The man had power. Over her, at least. Power that made her forget herself. Power that made it easy to forget that he was one of the richest men in the world. That he was one of the most sought after. That he was a man who could have anything he wanted. Any woman he wanted.

All the women he wanted.

A man like the one who had made her young life so difficult and devastated her mother's.

And that made Shane not only a risky proposition but someone Maya knew to keep away from. Especially when he could do to her what he'd done tonight with just the touch of his hand.

Four

Maya could have asked someone to drive her out to the McDermot ranch the next morning to wait for the mechanic to arrive to fix her mother's car. She didn't have to ride her old bicycle all the way there. But it was an exquisite spring day and she wanted the time to herself, mainly to realign a perspective that seemed to be going more and more askew every moment she spent with Shane.

The man had swept her off her feet the night before. There was no denying it. The simple touch of his hand, his kiss had made her lose track of why she needed to practice some restraint. Some resistance. They'd drawn her in, made her feel things she hadn't known she could feel, and raised in her such a longing for more that it scared the bejesus out of her.

It had left her sleepless. It had left her worried about the power he could wield over her without even trying. And she'd gotten out of bed at daybreak determined to get some control over herself and the situation.

That goal was aided by riding down Center Street and remembering who owned most of the buildings that lined it. It was aided by going past the lumber mill just outside town and seeing the big sign that proclaimed it the Heller Mill. It was aided by spotting the Heller house not too far beyond that.

Shane McDermot might have been one of the richest men in the world, but the Hellers were one of the founding families of Elk Creek and their stamp was on the small town at every turn.

Reminding herself of that was just what Maya needed. Reminding herself of Shag Heller was just what she needed.

Shag Heller. Father of Jackson, Linc and Beth. Uncle of Savannah and Ivey. Love of Margie's life.

Maya's own father had been killed in a hunting accident two months before she was born, leaving Margie with a small diner, a baby on the way and not much else. But Margie had worked hard to expand the diner, to make a go of it and to raise Maya on her own.

It wasn't a scenario Maya envied and she appreciated all her mother had done to accomplish it, to give her the happy, loving childhood she'd had.

At least the happy, loving childhood she'd had until she was twelve.

That was when Margie had fallen in love with the recently widowed Shag Heller.

And nothing had ever been the same after that.

Shag Heller had been a hard man with a stubborn streak a mile wide, and he'd had it in his head that his kids should never see him with a woman who wasn't their mother. So although he began to woo Margie, he insisted it be kept under wraps. A backdoor romance.

Unfortunately, being true to his wife's memory in his children's eyes and being true to Margie were two different things. His money and prestige had made him a sought-after commodity despite his difficult disposition, and he hadn't been faithful to Margie.

Still, Maya's mother had hung on. She'd accepted the relationship on his terms. She'd made all the sacrifices, all the compromises. Because she'd wanted to be the one he ultimately chose.

The trouble was, when Shag Heller had finally chosen, he hadn't chosen Margie. He'd chosen a woman he'd met in Denver after turning his ranch over to Jackson. And all Margie's waiting, all Margie's patience, all Margie's compromises, all Margie's tolerance had been for nothing.

Oh, sure, he'd settled enough money on Margie to make certain she would never want for anything financially, but he'd broken her heart. He'd nearly broken her spirit.

Maya had nursed her mother through what had been close to a nervous breakdown. She'd seen the emotional devastation. And holding her own mother in her arms when Margie collapsed after the relationship ended had made a harsh impact. It strengthened the resolves Maya had made while watching what went on between her mother and the wealthy rancher through her teenage years. And Maya had vowed there would be no Shag Hellers in her life.

But now there was Shane McDermot. And if ever there was anyone who could have anything he wanted, anyone he wanted, it was Shane. He was a rich and powerful man—even richer and more powerful than Shag had been. He was a man who had greener pastures outside every door. A man—like Shag Heller—who had a smorgasbord of life at his disposal. And an even bigger smorgasbord of women tracking him down, throwing themselves at him, willing to expose themselves or break into his house to be with him.

And Maya was terrified that Shane McDermot could be her Shag Heller.

So, no thanks, she thought. She was not going to let herself be as vulnerable as her mother had been. She was not going to compete with a whole world of women who wanted one certain man—a man who would expect to call all the shots with her because he could call all the shots with everyone else. A man who could, at any moment, indulge in the temptations that whole world of willing women offered, the same way he would indulge himself in anything else his little heart desired and leave her high and dry just as Shag Heller had left her mother.

And if the simple touch of Shane McDermot's hand could wipe out all thought, all reason...? Then she'd just have to avoid his touch so that she didn't end up losing sight of how it could end. She'd just have to avoid seeing him, being with him altogether.

Because when a man could have anything he wanted, the woman who wanted him was at a disadvantage. She was bound to get hurt. And Maya had no intention of letting anything like that happen to her.

No intention whatsoever.

But that was easier said than done when she rode up the drive to the McDermot house and found the hood of her mother's car up and Shane bent over the engine.

Steel yourself, she ordered silently, like a soldier on the front line.

She was far enough away that he didn't hear the quiet whir of the bicycle tires and so she got an eyeful of him before he knew she was approaching.

Her memory of Shag Heller didn't include whether or not he'd been attractive. He might have been—certainly his sons were—but in Maya's mind there was too much ugliness about his actions and the way he'd treated her mother to remember him as handsome enough to compare with Shane.

But then, to her, no one was handsome enough to compare with Shane. Not even his twin.

He had on a chambray shirt with the sleeves rolled to his elbows, exposing thick, sinewy forearms. A pair of tight, work-worn jeans rode a traffic-stopping derriere and careened down muscular thighs spread wide to brace himself as he reached far under the hood. And his mud brown cowboy boots looked as if they'd been around as many years as her mother's old car.

But even dressed without distinction, he was a sight to behold, and Maya did plenty of beholding all the way up the drive, even as she told herself that she really could resist him. She really could. She really could....

"Hi," she called as she finally drew near enough to be heard.

He turned his head in her direction without coming out from under the hood, and even in shadow, that first look at his face took her breath away. Rich, powerful and much, much too gorgeous—he was a lethal combination.

When he realized it was Maya who'd greeted him, he made a few more turns of a wrench and then pulled out from under the hood, straightening up to a full six feet two inches of the broad-shouldered, narrow-waisted, long-legged, masculine powerhouse he was.

"Why didn't you let me know you didn't have a ride out here? I could have picked you up," he said in answer to her gesture.

"I wanted the exercise," she said. When she came to a stop alongside the car, she nodded in the direction of the front end. "What are you doing in there?"

He grinned at her and that was all it took for her heart to skip a beat. "Fixin' it," he said simply.

"Fixing it? You mean you knew what was wrong and could have gotten it going last night?"

"Yep," he confessed without remorse.

"Then why didn't you?"

"And give up my excuse to drive you home?" he asked, as if she were out of her mind to even consider it. "Think I'm a fool?"

She probably should have been angry with him, she told herself. If he'd fixed the car the night before, she could have avoided the hand holding, the kiss, seeing him again today and all the things he had the ability to awaken inside her. But somehow she couldn't dredge up anger at any of it. Instead she got off the bicycle and basked in the warm, welcoming glow of his jade green eyes.

"So what was wrong with it?" she asked with another nod at the car's engine.

"Would you know what I was talkin' about if I told you?"

"No."

"Then why waste our time. Had breakfast?"

"Before I started out."

He released the bar holding the hood up and let it slam back into place. Then he took a rag he had sitting on the bumper and began to wipe his hands.

Now, how that could be erotic, Maya didn't know. But there he was, massaging an old, soiled cloth with greasy hands and into her mind flashed an instant fantasy of him kneading her body that same way. Of him squeezing, caressing, rubbing parts of her that had no business coming to life at that moment, out in his driveway in the light of day. But she could feel her breasts throb, her nipples kernel, her stomach tighten, her legs yearn to relax apart. And she couldn't help wondering if the rest of her might feel as incredible beneath his touch as her hand had felt the night before.

Tearing her eyes from the sight of his hands working that rag was one of the hardest things she'd ever done. And when she managed it, she found him watching her intently, curiously.

Don't blush. Don't blush, she ordered herself. But she could feel the heat working up from her neck. She swallowed with some difficulty and, hoping to keep him from seeing the blush, took her bicycle around to the trunk.

But she didn't have the key to open it. She'd left it with Shane the night before in case the mechanic arrived before she did today.

She cleared her throat to get words to pass through it and said, "Well, if you'll give me the key, I'll put this in the trunk and get out of your hair."

He just grinned at her again. "How 'bout at least havin' a cup of coffee before you run out of here?"

"No. Thanks. I'm working at the diner for the day while Mom has some beauty-shop time and does some shopping—it's part of my Mother's Day gift to her. So I need to get going."

"You would have been here longer if you had to wait for the mechanic to fix the car," he pointed out.

But Maya only responded to the reminder of the mechanic. "I need to go by the gas station and cancel that, too."

"Or you could just come inside and call."

"Don't you have work to do today?" she countered, feeling like a mouse being backed into a corner by a cat and deciding her only defense was a little offense.

"Some. But it can wait."

"Well, mine can't," she said in no uncertain terms, because she knew if she didn't get out of there soon she was going to be lost. She only seemed to have a small store of resistance to Shane at any one given time, and that hand-wiping thing had exhausted it, leaving her wanting to seize any reason to stay a while longer. To talk to him. To feast her eyes on him. To feel his touch again.

Which was exactly why she couldn't stay.

"The key?" she repeated, sounding slightly desperate to her own ears and hoping he'd missed it.

He shook his head, reached into his pocket for the key and said, "You are the damn toughest woman to pin down."

Visions of him pinning her down—with that long, hard body of his pressing her soft, pliant one into a downy mattress—flashed through her mind and lit tiny sparks that rained through her blood vessels.

"I just have things to do, places to go, people to see," she chattered, feeling like an idiot and not at all happy that among the things he could do to her, reducing her to blathering was one of them.

Shane used the key to open the trunk and lifted the bicycle inside for her. Then he closed it and held the key out to her.

She took it, careful not to connect with his hand when she did. "Thanks," she repeated. "Do I owe you for the car repair?"

That one quirky eyebrow shot upward toward his hairline. "Hmm. There's an interestin' idea. Now that you mention it, yes, you do."

He was clearly enjoying whatever prospects were going through his mind. But since it had been Maya who brought up the idea of payment, she had to go along with it and only hope he was calculating a monetary fee. "Okay. How much?"

"I'll have to take it under consideration. Only thing I know for sure is that it won't be money you owe me," he said, as if reading her thoughts.

There was also a wicked promise in his tone, and with her resistance spent, a little balloon of delight floated inside Maya that she tried futilely to hold down.

"Just let me know," she heard herself say, as if she were open to anything, when in fact she knew she should disabuse him of whatever notions he might have for exacting payment other than money.

But it was too late and she decided she'd better just get out of there before things got any worse.

Pretending to be in need of keeping to a tight schedule, she made a beeline for the driver's side and got in before Shane could do more than follow behind.

"Thanks again," she said through the open window.

Something about her quick goodbye—or maybe about her dash into the safety of the car—made him chuckle and shake his handsome head again. But all he said was, "Sure."

Then Maya started the engine—without any problem this time—waved and hit the gas so hard she left rubber on the drive as she peeled away.

Hardly a graceful exit, she realized. But Shane

McDermot was just too appealing and she couldn't tempt fate any more than she already had.

After thirty-four years in business, Margie Wilson's Café nearly ran itself. Minnie Shields could handle the cooking duties despite the fact that Margie did a fair amount of food preparation, and Mary Ellen Franklin did most of the waiting on tables unless some teenage help could be found. But the place needed at least one other person who could take care of the counter and the cash register and do some general overseeing. That was where Maya came in in place of her mother.

There was always a steady stream of customers, even between the breakfast, lunch and dinner rushes, because the only other restaurant options were the Dairy King for fast food and ice-cream confections or—on the one night a week when they served dinner—the local honky-tonk, the Buckin' Bronco. Over its long history, the diner had become as much a meeting place as an eating establishment, so some folks came in just for coffee, a slice of pie and a chat with friends.

Maya had been one of the after-school waitresses from the time she was old enough to do the job until she left for college, but she hadn't worked the café since then. Usually when she came home for a visit, Margie took time off and Maya steered clear of the restaurant to avoid seeing those few folks in Elk Creek she would rather not meet up with. But this trip, Margie was shorthanded and would only accept the gift of a day at the beauty salon and shopping if Maya agreed to help out.

It wasn't as bad as Maya had expected it to be, probably because by late that afternoon no one she minded seeing had yet come in. She was actually enjoying herself and the time she'd spent catching up with folks she liked and hadn't seen in more than a decade.

As she arranged place settings in anticipation of the supper crowd, the bell that hung over the door clattered an announcement of a customer. Maya glanced up to find that the woman who had just entered was not someone she knew. That had happened with about half her customers throughout the day, making her realize how much new blood Elk Creek had attracted since she'd been gone.

But not only was this particular woman unfamiliar to Maya, she didn't look like anyone who would be from Elk Creek at all. In fact, she looked as if she'd just stepped off the cover of a high fashion magazine. *If she's not a New York model, I'll eat my hat,* Maya thought as she took in the woman's appearance.

She was very tall—close to six foot if she was an inch—but she wasn't bowed by it. She held herself as straight as royalty awaiting the presentation of commoners. She was also reed thin beneath a blue leather suit made up of a tight, tight miniskirt and a short bolero jacket. Stylishly short blond hair framed a face blessed with ultrahigh cheekbones, flawless features and eyes so blue they almost didn't seem real.

There weren't many people in the café. Minnie and Mary Ellen were taking a coffee break together at the end of the counter, there were two men at one table and three women at another. But within moments of the newest customer's arrival, conversation fell into dead silence and every head turned her way. She was just that kind of woman.

"Hi," Maya greeted her without leaving the spot from which she was working. "Go ahead and sit anywhere you'd like. We aren't formal around here. Menus are on the tables and I'll be with you in a minute."

The woman turned her head slowly in Maya's direction as if she hadn't noticed her before. "I'm only trying to find someone who can give me directions," she said imperiously.

"That's easy enough. What are you looking for?" Maya asked.

"Shane McDermot's ranch."

Maya felt a little like she'd been slapped, though she couldn't for the life of her figure out why that should be so.

"You know Shane?" she heard herself ask with a tinge of challenge in her voice, not realizing she was going to say that, let alone in such a tone.

"We haven't met yet, no," the woman answered, as if it were inconsequential. Which it probably was, Maya thought, because one look at this woman and no doubt Shane would be thrilled at the chance to make her acquaintance.

"Is he expecting you?" Maya persisted, knowing she sounded like a door-guarding secretary but unable to help herself.

"No, he isn't." Again, inconsequential. "Can you tell me how to locate him?"

"Sorry. I can't." The words just came out on their own. With force and not too nicely, once more surprising Maya.

The response didn't please the other woman. She scanned the room. "Can anyone else tell me how to find Shane McDermot?"

Every eye in the place made a trip to Maya, as if she'd forbidden them all to speak and they weren't sure they should venture rebellion. Then, apparently deciding they shouldn't, they shook their heads in the negative and a few muttered sorrys and nos made the rounds. Everyone pretended to go back to what they'd been doing before the other woman came in, even though they were still casting surreptitious glances in her direction.

"Fine. I'll try somewhere else," she finally said tersely, turning on her two-inch heels and striding out on legs good enough to advertise hosiery.

Maya watched her go. Watched her through the plate glass front window all the way out onto the sidewalk and into the dry cleaner's next door.

And she felt absolutely rotten.

She tried to tell herself that something intangible about the woman had rubbed her wrong. She tried to tell herself that she was right not to have given her

directions to the McDermot ranch because Shane
would want his privacy protected.

But she didn't believe a bit of it.

How could she when she had the worst sinking feeling she'd ever had in her life?

She knew the woman would find someone to tell
her where Shane was. She knew the woman would
eventually meet up with him. And she knew the
woman would knock his socks off when he got one
glance at her.

After all, this was no trampy woman pulling up her
T-shirt to show him her breasts or marching up to his
front door in stiletto heels. This was no wacko who
would break into his house and get into a bed she
thought he was in. This was an incredibly beautiful,
classy woman any man alive would drool over. A
woman who made all other women—Maya included—
pale by comparison.

And even though she told herself she should be
glad, that this would be the ultimate distraction for
Shane, that once he set eyes on the other woman, he'd
never give Maya a second thought and she wouldn't
have to contend with any more of his charm, glad was
not how she felt. Not by any stretch of the imagination.

Because when it came right down to it, she was just
plain jealous.

By four-thirty the first wave of the dinner rush came
in the form of senior citizens. By five, most of the

tables were occupied and Maya had enough to do to take her mind off the beautiful woman looking for Shane. Almost. Almost enough to wipe out the mental images of what a stunning couple they would make.

That was when he showed up.

Actually, that was when he slipped into the restaurant like a secret agent, keeping his eyes trained outside until the door closed behind him, then casting a quick, searching glance through the front window.

Apparently satisfied, he finally spun on his heels and surveyed the room. His gaze only roamed as far as Maya. Once those iced jade eyes of his spotted her, they lit up and he headed for her like a heat-seeking missile.

She was behind the counter filling glasses with soda for one of Mary Ellen's orders, and although she froze for a moment when she saw him, she made sure she got right back to work. She was determined not to give in to any effect he might have on her. As determined as she was not to let him know he was having any effect at all.

"Sanctuary. I need sanctuary," he said when he reached the counter, sounding like a desperate, hunted man, albeit one who was at least partially enjoying it.

"Sorry. I don't think that's on the menu today," she said glibly but with an edge to her voice.

"Have a heart, woman. Some female's been doggin' me for the last hour and I'm afraid for my life," he joked in return. "Don't send me back out on those mean streets."

"Want to wait tables?" Maya goaded, wishing she wasn't so glad to see him that every sense was standing up and taking notice.

But before Shane could answer, the bell above the door jangled again and in came the model—as Maya had begun to think of the woman.

Shane took one look at her and did a swashbuckler's leap over the counter. Which was surprising enough in itself. But to compound Maya's shock, he grabbed her, pulled her into his arms and planted a great big kiss on her lips.

Then, when he'd finished claiming her with that kiss—and in a voice loud enough for the entire restaurant to hear—he said, "Hi there, cute stuff. Been a long day without you."

Maya's head was spinning, her mouth felt bee-stung and it took her a moment to gather her wits about her. Somewhere in the midst of all this, the model had made her way to the counter and stood witness to what Shane was doing. And what he was doing—with his arms still hooked around Maya's waist, looking down into her eyes—was making it seem as if they were a couple. Or so Maya realized a little late.

Only then did he seem to notice the other woman, giving her a chagrined smile. "What'd I tell you?" he said to the model. "Don't believe everything you read, 'cause I'm not as eligible as you think. In fact, I'm downright ineligible."

The other woman cast Maya a disdainful look and said disparagingly, "You'd rather have a *waitress?*"

"I'm also the cashier," Maya added out of orneriness, drawing a disgusted glance but no more acknowledgment than that.

"Yes, ma'am," Shane said enthusiastically to the other woman's question, "I'd rather have a waitress...and cashier. Thanks just the same."

The model took a business card from a compact purse and held it out to him. It was not just a plain business card, but more like a paper-thin engraved platinum name plate. "Think it over," she said confidently, raising a come-hither eyebrow. "You may change your mind."

"Not likely," he answered, keeping his arms around Maya rather than reaching for the card.

The other woman left it on the counter and gave him a smile that said she knew he'd come around sooner or later. Then she turned and glided out of the restaurant she'd once again turned stone-cold silent with her floor show.

When the bell clattered over her exit, Shane let Maya go, leaving her with a vague feeling of disappointment at losing even that mock embrace.

"What was all that?" she asked.

Shane grinned down at her, leaned in close enough so the rest of the place couldn't hear and said, "She wanted to mo-lest me—as Buzz puts it."

The business card had made Maya hope she'd been wrong in her own assumption of that same thing. She wasn't heartened to hear she'd been right all along.

"And you weren't interested?" she couldn't resist asking.

"In that ice queen? I saw her comin' a mile away and know her kind. She doesn't care whether it's a sweetheart or a sweat hog holdin' the wallet, 'long as it gets opened to pay for that designer suit she was wearin'. Thanks, but no thanks to that song and dance."

"And which are you? A sweetheart or a sweat hog?" Maya teased.

He winked at her. "Little of both, maybe."

Maya couldn't resist smiling at him. Or feeling better.

At least until he took the woman's card off the counter and put it in his pocket. Was he just getting it out of the way? she wondered. Or was he keeping it for future reference?

Jealousy reared its ugly head again but Maya tried hard to fight it. She didn't have any claim on this man, she told herself. She didn't *want* any claim on him. He could do as he liked. With the woman's card. With the woman. She didn't care.

Except that she did.

But Shane was oblivious to the turmoil inside her. Instead he made himself right at home by stepping to the sink at the end of the bar and washing his hands. Then he dried them on a towel next to it and turned back to Maya.

"So now that you've saved me from that black

widow spider, guess I'll need to do what I signed on for—table waitin'.''

"You're really going to wait tables?" Maya said dubiously, feeling a little of the jealousy ebb with the idea that he was trumping up this excuse to stick around.

"Better'n washin' dishes." He looked out at the café's clientele—who were all pretending not to watch what was going on behind the counter—and addressed them as a whole. "How 'bout it, folks? Be all right if I do some table waitin' to repay our Maya here for savin' my rump from that man-hunter?"

Everybody laughed and enough words of encouragement came in response to egg him on.

"See there? I've been hired on by popular demand," he said, grabbing a pitcher of ice water from the counter and moving out to fill glasses.

Maya watched him wend through the tables. He was dressed in better clothes than he'd had on when she'd seen him that morning—less worn jeans and a crisp hunter green western shirt that made the color of his eyes more pronounced. He knew a greater number of her customers than she did, calling everyone by name, asking about grandchildren, grain prices and gallbladders, and amusing them all with a heavy ladling of his laid-back charm and humor as he took orders and made jokes about his new job as headwaiter—a promotion he bestowed upon himself. Basically he worked the room as if he were the host of a big party.

And he stayed all the way till closing. All the way

till Minnie had finished in the kitchen and left. All the way till Mary Ellen had added up her receipts, stashed her apron in the laundry hamper and left with her tips—and his, too.

All the way till he was alone with Maya.

She locked the front door after Mary Ellen, flipped the Open-Closed sign so that Closed faced outside, and made a show of scanning up and down the street through the window.

"Looks like the coast is clear if you want to make a run for it," she told Shane as he ended his floor-sweeping chore and put the broom in the storage closet from which it had come.

"I'm thinkin' to be safe we'd better go out together. Never know where the man-eater might be lurkin'," he joked. "Besides, I couldn't go without helpin' right up to the end."

"This *is* the end," Maya informed him. "The kitchen is clean. The tables and the counter are set for breakfast. The floor is swept. And I'm ready to go home."

"I haven't seen that old car of your mother's any-where, back or front. How're you gettin' there?"

"I'm walking. Mom needed to use her car today, and even though she offered to pick me up tonight, I told her not to. I like to walk after working here—it helps get the food smells out of my hair."

"All right, then. Let's go. I'm parked at the medical building—had to have one of Buzz's prescriptions filled and that's where I left the truck. It's right on the way so I can walk you home.''

''My mother's house is only on the way if you make a big loop rather than crossing the town square to the medical building,'' she pointed out, even as an internal debate tore at her. One part of her was willing to grab at any reason to have him walk her home. The other knew it was better if they parted company right then and there.

''Can't chance going across that park. I might get jumped.''

''In Elk Creek?''

''Don't forget there's city women lurkin' around after me,'' he said with a grin, letting her know there wasn't a bit of truth to any of what he was pretending to be concerned about. He was merely fabricating more excuses for them to be together.

But since the part of her that had been arguing in favor of more togetherness seemed to have won out, Maya just conceded.

They went out the back door into the alley that ran behind the shops and businesses that lined Center Street. Each building kept a light on so it wasn't dark, and since everyone in town took pride in keeping things nice—even the alley—it was a neat and presentable walkway.

It wasn't paved, though, so the sound of their footsteps on the pebbled path seemed to echo off the buildings. To Maya it accentuated the fact that they suddenly weren't talking, and the silence made her uncomfortable.

"So. Shall I tell Mom to expect her new headwaiter for the breakfast rush tomorrow morning?" she teased just to have something to say.

"Will you be there?" he asked.

"No, this is my only turn as a waitress—"

"And cashier," he reminded.

"And cashier. But you seemed to cotton to the job. I thought maybe you'd want it as a new career."

He pretended to consider the possibility before saying, "Think maybe I'll stick with ranchin' just the same."

The small talk died and he didn't seem inclined to search for more. He appeared content to just walk along together in the cool May night, his chin slightly raised as if he were enjoying the smell of the clean spring air.

But Maya was all too aware of him so close beside her. Of the pure size of him—tall and perfectly built. Of the way he kept his steps slow so she didn't have to struggle to match the stride of long legs. Of his profile in the moonlight—chiseled and heart-stoppingly handsome in his unconventional, ruggedly masculine way.

And she needed a distraction.

"Tell me about that new breed of cow you said you and Ry wanted to try out—the reason you guys took over Buzz's ranch rather than staying in Texas with the rest of your family," she said, seizing the only thing she could think of to talk about. "Did it work out for you or not?"

He chuckled deep in his chest, a sound that made goose bumps skitter across her skin for no reason she could fathom.

"It worked out," he said in understatement. "One bull I brought back from a trip to Europe started what *Prominence Magazine* called my cattle *empire*." He ended that with self-deprecation but Maya suspected that an empire was just what it had started.

"What was so great about that one bull?" she asked.

"Ah, he was a beauty," Shane breathed with the kind of admiration only a cowboy could have. "I got him in France, and Ry and I put him to stud right away. He was hardy as they come. Calved well—his offspring can live even if they're born in the dead of winter. And the beef that comes from them…you'll never taste better. Nobody will. That's why there's such a high demand for it."

Maya couldn't help laughing at him as they turned onto Third Street and her mother's house came into view four doors from the corner.

"What?" he asked, obviously not understanding what she found funny.

"I've never heard anyone get so rapturous over a cow."

Shane smiled at her, heating up her blood with just that glance. "That old boy was worthy of rapture," he defended himself good-naturedly. "Buried him standin' up when he took his last breath."

That really made her laugh. "You buried him? Standing up? I suppose he has a headstone, too?"

"You bet your birthdays he does. We all took the day off work, had a service, paid him the respect he was due."

"I'm sorry," Maya apologized for laughing out loud, although Shane didn't seem to take offense. He just grinned, too.

"Are you makin' fun of me, Miss Smart Britches from the big city now?"

"No. I just can't help it. I have this picture in my head of you holding a funeral for a cow," she said between ripples of laughter she couldn't seem to escape.

"For a *bull*," he corrected. "He was a bull. Best there ever was."

"Excuse me. A funeral for a *bull*."

They'd reached her mother's small frame house by then and Shane walked a still-laughing Maya all the way up onto the wide front porch, where a light was burning for her return. Maya knew the door wouldn't be locked so she didn't bother with a key. Instead she faced Shane when she'd finally gotten her mirth under control—something that was easier to do when she realized that this put an end to her time with him.

"Think you'll be safe getting the rest of the way to your truck?" she teased him.

"I don't know. Maybe I should stay over till daybreak," he suggested with a wicked wiggle of his brows as he gazed down into her eyes.

"Sorry. Mom doesn't allow sleepovers."

"Too bad. Guess I'll have to chance it, then."

Maya nodded, ending in an upward angle that left her unintentionally staring into his light-gilded features.

"Well, I suppose this is good-night," she said in a voice oddly husky all of a sudden.

"Not quite yet. I decided on my payment for fixin' your mother's car this mornin'," he said with a touch of mischief creeping into his expression.

"And what would that be?"

"A kiss," he answered, as if it were a challenge.

"I'll call Mom out here and tell her," she joked, reaching for the handle on the screen door.

Shane laughed and caught her wrist before she made it all the way to the knob. "Not from Margie," he elaborated unnecessarily, pulling Maya ever so slightly nearer.

She thought she should probably put up more of a protest, but somehow she just couldn't think of one. She could only peer into those gorgeous green eyes and let herself be carried away into their depths.

And truth to tell, he didn't give her much time for denial before he leaned in and actually did kiss her. Just a trial kiss. As if it weren't a keeper.

But then the keeper came close behind.

He let go of her wrist and wrapped his arms around her to ease her close to him as his lips parted over hers. One hand cradled her head as he deepened the kiss even more, urging her lips to part, too.

Not that she required much encouragement. At that moment it seemed as if kissing Shane had been all that was on Maya's mind since early that morning when she'd seen him bent over the car engine. Maybe all that had been on her mind since the night before, when he'd barely bussed her. It was as if the craving for his kiss had been just below the surface that whole time, in a way she hadn't even been aware of.

But she was aware of it now. Aware of needs rising up inside her with an intensity that made her light-headed and of a yearning to give herself over to the man, to his kiss.

And give herself over to it she did.

When his mouth opened even more, she opened hers in answer. She even let arms that were aching to be around him, hands that were itching to press against his broad, hard back have their way.

All thoughts about the danger she was courting with him, about the other women who were clamoring for him, about her own determination not to be among them, not to compete or risk all that being with a man like him risked, were quieted and shoved to the back of her mind.

There was just that one moment. That kiss. The bliss of having her breasts against his hard, honed chest. Of having the velvety warmth of his mouth over hers. Of his tongue barely teasing the dip her upper lip took in the center. Of breathing in that faint, lingering scent of his aftershave. Of feeling the roughness of his late-day beard against her skin. Of yielding to the mastery of him.

And if there had been some deeper meaning in the touch of their hands the night before, the same was there in their kiss. A sense that the connection they were making was preordained. Meant to be. That two halves of the same whole were finally coming together....

But just as she was completely, totally lost in that kiss, in Shane, in the strange sensation that they were being drawn to each other by some force greater than either of them, he ended it. Not all at once, but slowly. Kissing her yet again a time or two or three, before he seemed to actually be able to stop.

He laid his forehead to hers and kissed the tip of her nose, playfully.

"Got any more cars need fixin'?" he joked in a deep, raspy voice that let her know that the power of that keeper kiss—of the connection they'd made—had rocked him, too.

"Sorry," she whispered, wishing she had a whole fleet of vehicles he could work on if she got kissed like that in the guise of payment for services rendered.

But little by little Maya regained herself and remembered all the reasons she shouldn't be indulging in kissing with him, remembered—most especially—that he'd taken the other woman's card from the counter and put it in his pocket.

It lent her a renewed resolve and she pulled as far away as he'd let her. "I need to go in."

He sighed but didn't try to stop her. Instead his arms fell away, allowing her to step back.

"I'll see you tomorrow night, then," he said.

"Tomorrow night?"

"We're havin' a party out at the ranch for Buzz. He wanted to get everybody over to let them know he's back in town. As if anyone didn't know already. I called your mom today and talked to her. She accepted for you both."

Of course she did, Maya thought, feeling again that whatever was going on between them was out of her control.

Shane seemed to read her mind and he pressed a long index finger to her lips. "Too late for excuses. You're comin'," he decreed.

Then he took his finger away and kissed her one last time—a kiss that was somewhere between the passion-filled one and those scant final pecks.

"'Night, Miss Maya," he said quietly afterward. "I had myself one hell of a good time with you tonight."

He didn't wait for her to answer. He just turned and did a hop-skip down the three porch steps and into the night, leaving her wondering why the Fates were torturing her with temptation in the form of the handsome, charming, funny, sexy Shane McDermot. Who she knew, as surely as she knew her own name, couldn't be good for her.

Five

As Shane stood in front of the bathroom mirror the next evening to shave after showering off the day's work grime, it took him a minute to get his left eye to focus.

That happened sometimes. But his vision always adjusted itself. It was no big deal. Just a minor nuisance left over from the accident he'd had four years ago. He could live with it. Better an occasional blur than what it might have been.

Besides, it served as a reminder to him. An especially welcome reminder now, when he seemed to be having a lot of trouble keeping some things in mind.

He blinked repeatedly until he could see clearly again, then leaned over the sink to study the scar that zigzagged up into his brow—the scar that went hand in hand with the periodic blurred vision.

Maybe it would have been better if the scar hadn't healed over so well, he thought. If he'd been left more marked. Not that he wanted to be disfigured. He didn't. No one did. But maybe if the scar was just slightly more pronounced, it would act as the catalyst it had been four years ago. The kind of catalyst the accident itself had been.

Shane pushed away from the mirror and lathered the lower portion of his face, thinking that it was good that he, at least, could see the scar, because what had gone on after that accident had taught him a lesson. The hard way. A lesson he didn't ever want to have to learn again.

Maybe that was why his vision had fogged up just now. Why he'd noticed the scar. Maybe his subconscious was planting the reminder at that particular moment because he was on the verge of going head over heels the way he had four years ago. Of losing his edge where Maya was concerned.

And maybe he needed some reminding to maintain that edge so he wouldn't get burned again.

But not even the reminder of the accident and what had come afterward was helping, he realized as he shaved white foam from under his nose. Because he was still as eager as a new pup to get Maya out to the ranch for the party. Eager to see her. To talk to her. To touch her. To kiss her again.

But the reminder did leave him wondering why it was so tough to keep the emotional distance from her that he'd learned to keep from other women until he got to know them, until he knew whether they had any substance to them or if they were as shallow as many of the women he ran into. As shallow as Penny had been.

Maybe it was because Maya wasn't *other women,* he thought, although he couldn't really pinpoint what it was that struck him as so different.

There was just something about her that drew him like a magnet. That had him thinking about her day and night. Something that pulled him to wherever he knew she'd be—like yesterday's hiding-out at the café. Something that had him hungry for her company and more hot and bothered with wanting her than he'd been in a long, long time.

And it wasn't only that he was crazy about the way she looked. Although he was. He loved her natural-ness. Her lack of artifice. He loved that long, sleek hair; that alabaster skin; those great big doe eyes that sparkled when she smiled; that tight, compact body that lit a fire inside him every time he got near her.

But that wasn't all there was to it for him. He also loved just being with Maya. Hearing the sound of her voice. Making her laugh the way he'd done the night before. He couldn't pinpoint exactly what it was he felt. But when he was with her it was like pulling on a favorite pair of jeans, jeans he'd worn for so many years they seemed to have memorized the shape of him. It just felt right. It felt like a perfect fit. Inside and out.

So how did a man resist someone like that? he asked himself. How did he keep his edge with her when every inclination was to throw caution to the wind? To plunge right in?

Maybe just by remembering, he thought with an-other glance up toward the scar again. By remember-ing and by being careful.

But in the process he could get to know her, get to

know what made her tick, what was important to her, and use that to figure out how big a risk he might be taking if he became involved with her. He could go on reminding himself to keep his eyes open, not to jump in with both feet until he knew more, to hold as many of his feelings under lock and key as he could.

But even as he embraced that idea, he had his doubts about it. Not about keeping his eyes open. But when he was with Maya, it was nigh on to impossible for him not to jump in with both feet. And he didn't think there was a lock and key big enough to contain the feelings she stirred up inside him.

Still, he had to try, he told himself. He had to try damn hard if he was going to let himself get anywhere near her.

Let himself get anywhere near her? That was a laugh.

Because near her was just where he was champing at the bit to be. It was where he couldn't stop himself from being any more than he could stop himself from breathing.

He just hoped to hell he could hang on to his heart when he got there. But reminders or no reminders, he wasn't too sure he could.

"I wish you'd worn something a little more festive. And feminine."

"I didn't bring anything more festive or more feminine with me," Maya told her mother as they got into Margie's car that evening to go to Buzz's party. Maya had on a pair of brown pin-striped trousers with a short-sleeved, mock-turtleneck sweater tucked into them. It was the most festive—and feminine—thing she'd packed.

Not that she'd have dressed to please her mother even if she had brought other clothes. Margie had spent their day together urging Maya to set her cap for Shane McDermot. Maya had spent it trying to convince her mother—and maybe herself—that she just wasn't interested in the man. And there was no way she would have made a lie of that—or tempted the Fates more than she already had—by wearing something suggestive.

Although it was a tempting, titillating fantasy.

"Who all do you think will be here tonight?" Maya asked to change the subject as Margie headed up Center Street toward the town square and the road that would take them to the McDermot ranch.

But as her mother began to rattle off names, relationships and anecdotes to go with them, Maya's mind wandered.

She'd been having trouble concentrating all day. Instead her thoughts seemed to have a will of their own, roaming constantly to Shane. And to a countdown of how many more hours until she'd be with him again. How many more minutes…

If there was a way to resist the man's allure, she hadn't yet discovered it. And that scared her almost as much as her feelings about him did. And the fear was growing apace with her attraction to him—and how much more she liked him with every moment they were together.

If only he could be less handsome, she thought for the hundredth time that day. If only he could be less masculine. If only he could have a voice like a cartoon mouse or dirty fingernails or smelly feet or some annoying trait that would make her skin crawl.

But no. He had to be terrific. Terrific looking. Terrifically entertaining. Terrifically sweet and nice. Terrifically sexy. Terrific in every way.

And she was so bowled over by it all that she kept having these silly feelings that they somehow belonged together—as if it had been preordained by a force greater than either of them. A force that wiped out all reason, all rational thought, all common sense and wisdom the moment she saw him.

Well, not tonight, she thought forcefully, as if to warn off whatever that greater force might be.

She hadn't wanted to go to this party in the first place. She didn't want to socialize with people she'd avoided since high school. She didn't want to witness any more aggressive women in pursuit of Shane. And she didn't want to be swept off her feet again by the man himself.

"Are you sure we have to do this?" Maya asked her mother suddenly. "Couldn't we claim one of us got sick at the last minute and we had to stay home?"

Margie gave her a disparaging look. "It'll be fun," she said, daring Maya to let it be anything else.

Maya just closed her eyes, wondering how she was going to get through this evening.

"Here we are," Margie announced moments later, and when Maya opened her eyes, the McDermot house was coming into view right in front of her.

A welcoming white glow flooded the surrounding area from several porch lights as well as from the tall, wrought-iron pole lights with large white globes that lined the drive. And as she stared at the big, impressive house Shane had built, she told herself she didn't have to succumb to whatever it was that was going on between the two of them. That she really could fight it.

Couldn't she?

Determined that she could, she shored up her defenses and swore to herself that tonight she was going to resist him. No matter what it took.

And she meant it, too.

But as she got out of the car after her mother had parked it at the end of the long row of vehicles, Maya only hoped her resolve was strong enough. Because deep down she knew she was as susceptible to Shane as a sponge was to water.

And already—just walking up to his door—her heart was racing, nerve endings were alive, and all she wanted to do was be back in those same arms in which she'd ended the night before....

"It'll be just fine. Everything will be just fine," Margie said as if she sensed Maya's concerns. Then she rang the doorbell and there was nothing Maya could do but hope her mother was right.

Junebug opened the door in answer to the bell. She had a glass in hand and appeared to be acting as hostess. The formidable housekeeper said hello to Maya and then hugged Margie.

As the older women began to chat, Maya looked beyond the entryway, past the partygoers who were lingering there and into the expansive living room. She doubted that anyone in town *hadn't* been invited, and apparently few had declined to come. Not that it was surprising, since Buzz was a well-liked curmudgeon. Still, it only took Maya a split second to locate Shane in the crowd.

He stood a head taller than the group he was with. His hip-hugging black jeans were stretched taut through the legs by powerful thighs, and he wore a white western shirt with silver tips on the collar points. His sun-streaked hair looked freshly combed, his handsome face was clean-shaven, and his sleeves were rolled to his elbows, exposing thick forearms. Altogether he looked magnificent, and appreciation rippled through Maya like a tidal wave, leaving her feeling so weak she wasn't sure she could stay standing.

As if he were watching for her arrival, he glanced toward the front door and spotted her. His iced jade eyes lit up as his supple mouth stretched into a slow, private smile.

Maya read an ''Excuse me'' on his lips and he made his way toward her.

"Who's here?" she heard Buzz call from somewhere not far away.

Junebug paused in her conversation with Margie to holler back the information.

"Well, git on in here and say hello to me, little Maya," Buzz called in response.

Maya decided it was better to find the old man than to stand there waiting with bated breath for his grandson to reach her, so she followed the sound of Buzz's voice and discovered him ensconced in a big armchair just inside the arch that connected the living room with the entryway.

His bad leg was elevated on a matching leather hassock and the metal skeleton of his walker was on one side of him, so Maya stepped up to the other side. He took her hand as soon as she was near enough for him to reach it and pulled her closer still, poking a bony cheek up at her.

"Give a ol' man a kiss hello," he ordered.

Maya laughed at him and obliged. "How are you doing, Buzz?"

"Havin' a high ol' time gittin' to see everybody 'n 'er brother. How's come you come all the way out here yesterdee and didn't come in to see me? They coulda been starvin' me, you know. Or had me trussed up er somethin', an' you'da never know'd the difference."

"What did I tell you about spinnin' those yarns to someone who's supposed to be checkin' on you, Buzz?"

It was Shane's voice that came from behind Maya and wrapped around her like a lover's arms. But she tried to hang on to her determination to resist him tonight and didn't so much as glance in his direction, staying focused on Buzz instead, who still held her hand.

The elderly man giggled in delight. "She knows by now I'm jus' funnin' with 'er. Would somebody bein' treated rotten have a git-together like this throw'd fer 'im?"

"I only stopped by yesterday to pick up Mom's car," Maya finally explained. "Then I needed to get over to the café to work."

"Coulda least said hey and brightened a borin' mornin'. Maybe it woulda set me to whistlin' the rest of the day the way it did the boy here."

Shane had stepped up beside her by then and Maya knew it was rude to go on not so much as glancing at him, especially when Buzz was making references to him. She finally looked up, finding him not the least embarrassed by his grandfather's comment, but instead grinning down at her as if he were so delighted to see her, nothing else mattered.

"Hi there, cute stuff," he greeted her in a tone as intimate as if they were alone. And just that quick, down came the walls of resolve she'd erected.

"Hi," she answered, and her eyes snagged on his and stuck for a time before Buzz broke the spell.

"Don't jes' stand there starin', boy. Take the girl to git a drink. An' a plate of food."

"Yes, sir," Shane said, as if accepting a command from a drill sergeant.

Buzz lifted Maya's hand to pass it to his grandson, and Shane didn't hesitate to take it.

Okay. Well. Having him hold her hand was definitely not helping matters. Sparks flew and ignited that magic once again at just his touch, making Maya even weaker than she had been before. But no power on earth could force her to pull free of him and she ended up being led into the dining room as if she'd completely lost a will of her own.

Luckily once they got there—where an enormous buffet was set out and a well-stocked bar waited to meet every imaginable taste—Shane let go of her hand to pour her a glass of the wine she'd agreed to without really thinking about it.

"Anybody in here you don't know?" he asked as he poured.

It was the first Maya became aware that there were other people around. She discovered plenty of them as she turned to the buffet table, where they all helped themselves to a delectable selection of Junebug's cooking.

There were some people she didn't recognize, but suddenly she was face-to-face with the two women she'd spent eleven years avoiding, and that was all she could think about.

"Don't worry, Shane honey, she knows us," Suzy Teeblat said smugly. Then she added with disdain, "Hello, Maya."

"Suzy."

"We heard you were in town," Suzy's cohort, Marcy Lumbly, put in. She tossed a meaningful glance from Maya to Shane and back again, then said under her breath to Suzy, "Some things never change, do they?"

"Like mother, like daughter," Suzy confirmed. Then, making no sound at all, she mouthed elaborately, "Gold-digging tramp."

"You're right about one thing," Maya shot back. "Some things—and some people—never do change. Especially not for the better."

Shane had turned from the bar by then and stepped up next to her with two wineglasses in one hand and two empty dinner plates in the other. But Maya didn't accept either a glass or a plate. It was bad enough to once again be insulted by her two worst childhood tormentors, but she couldn't stomach the sudden change in their attitudes as they became Misses Sweetness and Light to fawn over Shane, making it clear they were as much in pursuit of him as the woman on the train, the one in the stiletto heels and the model in the café the day before.

Besides, the whole incident had destroyed her appetite, and all Maya could think to do was get as far away from them as possible.

"I need some air," she said. And out she went, into the kitchen and through the back doors onto the patio.

The entire cobbled patio was roofed and surrounded by spindled poles, rails and posts that matched the verandas of both of the bedroom wings. She went as far as she could away from the house and leaned a shoulder against a corner pole, taking deep breaths of cool May air and thinking she might just stay there until her mother was ready to go home and came looking for her.

"What happened in there?"

Of course Shane had followed her, but she wished he hadn't. She wished she could just be alone. Wished she wasn't even in Elk Creek.

How did her mother stand it? Maya wondered. Living here. Facing people like Suzy Teeblat and Marcy Lumbly, who couldn't let anything die, even after all these years?

Maya didn't answer Shane's question. Instead she said, "Don't let me keep you from your guests."

He crossed to her anyway, resting his hips on the railing and facing the house while she stared out at the pool, which wasn't yet filled, and the big barn beyond it.

"Seein' to fresh claw marks left on one of my guests by two others of 'em is part of bein' a good host, isn't it?" he joked tenderly.

Maya wasn't too sure how much he'd heard or seen, but apparently it had been enough to know how catty Suzy and Marcy had been.

"No claw marks," she claimed. "I'm fine."

"Nope," he said simply, leaving her to wonder if he was denying that she was unscathed or if he was still refusing to go back to the party. "You know, those two felines are not Ry's and my favorite Elk Creek citizens, either.''

He'd piqued her curiosity. ''They were cheerleaders in high school and prom and homecoming queens— very popular. Most guys would have fallen all over themselves for them—although I understand 'they haven't had as much luck with the male gender since then. But still, I'd think two healthy men like you and Ry would find them pretty intriguing.''

''Ha! They're joined at the hip and they've been lettin' it be known for some time that gettin' together with us—and they don't seem to care which of us goes with which of them, as if we're interchangeable— would make for a perfect foursome. Like we're some kind of package deal they'd like to sign up for. And they're just plain nasty to everybody but Ry and me. They once nearly filleted poor Junebug for not tellin' them where we were when we were dodgin' them.''

The thought of *anyone* getting the better of Junebug made Maya smile at the absurdity of it. ''Junebug would squash them like little spiders.''

''You'd be surprised. They hurt her feelings. Told her she was nothin' but a fat old toilet-cleaner who needed to do the job she was bein' paid for and answer her *betters* when she was asked a question. Only reason they're here tonight is because Buzz doesn't know about it and gave out a blanket invitation to their families. And even then, me and Ry and Junebug thought about banning them from the place. But we decided to just ignore them and let Buzz have his party in peace."

Shane paused, and from the corner of her eye, Maya saw him give her a sidelong glance. "Seems like maybe ignorin' them comes easier for us than for you, though."

"It shouldn't. I've had a lot more years of practice."

Shane just let that lie for a while, waiting, maybe, for Maya to explain. When she didn't, he couldn't seem to contain his curiosity.

"You know, Buzz'll tell me whatever it is that's goin' on between you and those two cats when I ask him tomorrow. But I'd rather hear it from you."

Buzz would probably know, too, Maya thought. Gossip was the perfume in the air of a small town, and no doubt everyone knew not only about her mother's relationship with Shag, but also about the hell Suzy and Marcy had made of Maya's life over it. And if she told the story herself, it would buy her time to stay outside, away from them.

"My mother had a long-term affair with Shag Heller. I don't know if you've heard about it or not. It happened before you came here."

"Shag Heller..." He repeated the name as if trying to place it. "Is that Linc, Jackson and Beth's late father?" When Maya nodded, he said, "No, I haven't heard much about him except that he was a contrary old cuss who wasn't quite as mean as his brother, Ivey and Savannah's late father."

"That about sums them up."

"And Margie was involved with Shag Heller?"

"Not openly. But she was definitely involved with him." Maya went on to outline the whys and wherefores of her mother's backdoor romance. "It looked bad—the way Shag went about it," she continued. "Folks—me included, I'm ashamed to admit—wondered why Shag wasn't up-front about what was going on between him and Mom unless they were doing something to be ashamed of. Why didn't he openly court her unless he thought she wasn't good enough to be seen with him? Why did he act as if he were cheating on his dead wife unless something smarmy was going on? And what kind of woman would accept being treated like that?"

"You thought that of your mother?"

"I'm not proud of it. But yes, there was some of that in my thinking as I was growing up."

"And there were Suzy and Marcy to rub it in," he guessed.

"Every single day. They said Mom was a gold digger. And a tramp. And a whore…and every other awful name they could think of. They said she'd do anything, accept anything, because she wanted to get her hands on his money, because she thought if she did what he wanted, he'd marry her, but that decent men never married women like that and she was just a stupid fool to think otherwise."

"Sounds like a lot of that had to have come from home. Most kids don't say things like that."

"A lot of the people around town didn't approve of what was going on. Mom suffered the slings and arrows and—mostly—the cold shoulders of the adults. I got the runoff that came from their kids."

"But Margie didn't care?"

Maya shrugged. "Some of what they said was true—Mom did think if she let the relationship be on Shag's terms he'd eventually marry her. But not for his money. She loved him. Only to everyone else it didn't look like love. It looked like something much uglier than that."

Maya straightened her shoulders, a reflex that had started early on when the taunts had begun. "Lowlife scum—that was one of the favorites," she said, remembering it as if it were yesterday. "And the general consensus was that I wouldn't grow up to be any better."

"Must have been tough on you," Shane said with genuine compassion and a troubled frown she caught out of the corner of her eye. "How did it end—with your mother and Shag Heller?"

Maya told him about Shag leaving her mother for another woman.

"Which probably didn't help the talk any," he said when she'd finished.

"Made it seem like it was all justified. That of course he'd left her because she wasn't good enough for him. That we were just the town rabble, and no Heller would actually link up with us in any honorable way."

Shane groaned at that, shaking his head. "Not many things worse than being the scourge of a small town. I'm surprised Margie didn't pack up and leave."

"We couldn't do that. This was where her livelihood was. Selling the restaurant wouldn't have brought more than a pittance, and what could she do anywhere else? Be a short-order cook? We had to stay. Well, Mom felt as if she had to stay—"

"But you didn't."

"I left as soon as I could. To go to college. But Mom still wouldn't leave. She said this was her hometown and the talk would die down. I think it has for her."

"But Suzy and Marcy—"

"Still get too much of a kick out of needling me," Maya finished for him.

"And did Shag Heller marry the other woman?"

"No. But she didn't live here, and so it somehow seemed more aboveboard, I guess. Mom was right under everybody's nose—grist for their mill as the person who had let Shag Heller have his way with her without making an honest woman of her," Maya concluded with mock-melodramatic flourish.

"So you left to get away from it all and now pretty much stay away."

Maya nodded her confirmation of that.

"But here you are now."

"This is just a visit, with a little work thrown in. And ordinarily I keep a lower profile than this trip seems to be allowing me."

"Want me to go in and tell Suzy and Marcy to leave?" he offered. "Believe me, it would be my pleasure."

Maya laughed. "And make a scene that would ruin Buzz's party? No."

"Then how 'bout I keep you tucked under my arm the rest of the night so they can't get to you without goin' through me?"

Tucked under his arm...that was much too appealing a thought.

"I think I can manage all right. They just caught me off guard. But they won't get a second chance at me tonight. Or maybe I'll just poke their eyes out if they come anywhere near me," she joked feebly.

"I'll hold them down for you if you need me to," he joked back.

"Thanks."

The patio doors opened just then and Junebug stuck her head out. "There you two are. Got folks lookin' for you both. Come on in here," she said, as if they were recalcitrant children being taken to task.

Shane leaned over as if to whisper to Maya but said in a voice loud enough for Junebug to hear, "If we don't mind her, she's likely to come drag us in by the ears."

Maya raised her chin in agreement and pushed away from the pole. "We're coming," she told Junebug over her shoulder.

But the other woman apparently didn't trust them

because she stayed in the doorway until they actually did go in.

Kansas and Tallie were looking for Maya, Ry was looking for Shane, and so they were separated for about half an hour. But after that, Shane wasn't far from Maya's elbow through the rest of the evening.

And the rest of the evening wasn't as bad as its beginning.

With Shane acting as guard-at-the-gate to ward off Suzy and Marcy with some of the fiercest looks Maya had ever seen, they kept their distance. Even the Hellers were more friendly than they had been in years gone by—apparently having conquered the awkwardness their father's actions had made them all feel. And Maya discovered that with some of the tension taken away, she could relax around them, too. Kansas and Tallie helped make the party fun for her, but the real reason it wasn't a complete disaster was due to Shane.

And not only because he ran interference. He treated her like royalty while sharing wicked asides and private jokes with her. He brought her up to date on the lives of folks she'd known long ago and introduced her to those she hadn't met. It also didn't hurt that he made sure her wineglass was never empty, because the liquor put her more at ease.

It wasn't until very late, after Buzz had said goodnight to everyone and gone to bed and a large portion of the guests had left, that Maya began to search futilely for her mother among the remaining faces, thinking it was time for them to call it a night, too.

"Margie left, if that's who you're lookin' for," Shane informed her when it became obvious what she was doing.

"She left without me?"

"She motioned me over about an hour ago and asked if I'd take you home. Said not to tell you until after she'd gone or you'd leave with her and she didn't want you to. I didn't want you to, either, so I did as I was told."

Maya made a face and shook her head in amazement at her mother's unsubtle matchmaking tactics.

"Is that a bad thing?" he asked.

"I'm just sorry she put you on the spot. With what you have going on here, you shouldn't have to take me all the way into town."

"*All the way* into town? First, it's only a fifteen-minute drive. And second, I'd be happy to take you *all the way* anywhere, anytime, anyhow. You just let me know when you're ready," he said with an innu-endo-laden tone and a wink.

Maya laughed and tried not to notice the enticing possibilities that flashed through her mind at the thought of going *all the way* with Shane. "I can wait to go home until the party is over. I wouldn't want to drag one of the hosts away prematurely," she assured him, purposely ignoring the double entendres he'd tossed out.

But she didn't have much longer to wait to leave. Once the exodus had begun, it continued in a steady stream, and by midnight Ry was convincing Junebug that the mess would get cleared the next day—without her services since it was Mother's Day—and that she should go home, get to bed and not worry about it.

Then Ry said good-night and headed for bed, and Maya and Shane were alone.

"I wouldn't mind helping you clean up a little if you want to get a head start on things," she told him as she surveyed the debris.

"Nah. We have a crew of high school home economics kids set to come over in the mornin' to do most of the work. They're gettin' extra credit and pay to boot. We just didn't tell Junebug or she would've had a fit thinkin' we were payin' somebody else to do her work—at least that's how she'd look at it. So we kept it on the q.t." He grinned like an ornery boy caught at mischief. "Besides, she'll be pleased as punch thinkin' Ry and I aren't helpless without her."

"I guess you can take me home, then."

He didn't put up an argument the way she thought he might—maybe the way she *hoped* he might—to prolong their time together. Instead he just agreed and they headed out of the house through the back because he said all the cars and trucks were parked in the garage.

As they passed the spot where they'd talked earlier, they both glanced in that direction, as if recalling how the party had begun for Maya and all she'd confided in Shane. Neither of them said anything about it—at least not right then. But after he'd opted for driving his truck, which conveniently had a stack of papers and file folders on the passenger's side and kept Maya in the center of the bench seat next to Shane, he said, "So, has the stuff that went on with your mother and Shag Heller had anything to do with you not marryin' yet?"

"It isn't as if I've been proposed to a dozen times and turned every one of them down because of it, no."

"Once or twice maybe?"

"Not even that," she said, slightly embarrassed that she'd never had a relationship that had gone that far.

Shane gave her a penetrating once-over and then nodded to himself, as if he'd seen all he needed to.

"You keep everybody at arm's length, don't you?" he guessed.

"I'm careful about who I let get close, if that's what you mean," she admitted, surprised at herself for being even that candid.

"You keep 'em at arm's length," he said, as if he were suddenly sure of it.

"I haven't kept you at arm's length," she blurted out defensively. And unintentionally.

He grinned over at her with pure devilry in his expression. "You've tried. But it hasn't worked because I'm different from most men," he said with an exaggerated show of ego.

"Is that so?"

"Yes, ma'am. I'm one of the world's most eligible bachelors, you know."

What she knew was that they had reached her mother's house and he'd pulled to a stop at the curb.

She also knew she was still enjoying herself—enjoying him—too much to want it to end. And that she was much too aware of his thigh running the length of hers, and the sight of his big hands on the steering wheel, and the scent of his aftershave, and the warmth his body gave off to heat her to the core with a sensual flush.

"There's a whole world full of eligible bachelors," she pointed out to tease him.

He wiggled both his brows at her comically. "But I'm one of the top twelve."

He didn't mean for that to be taken seriously and it was a good thing, because the way he said it made Maya laugh.

"And even bein' one of those top twelve, you still would have kept me at arm's length if I'd have let you—the way a lesser man might have."

"But you're not a lesser man," she finished for him in the same joking vein.

"Want to find out for yourself?" he offered with a heavy dose of lasciviousness.

"I don't think so," she answered, laughing again.

"You just want to go up to your house wonderin'?"

"Wondering is good."

"Nah. Better to know these things," he said with certainty as he took her by the shoulders and turned her enough to face him.

He kissed her then. A showcase kind of a kiss that didn't seem for real at all.

And when he'd finished, Maya shook her head sadly and said, "Sorry, I've had better."

His grin was a slow stretch with pure orneriness around the edges. "Oh, you're askin' for it."

He was right, she was. And she knew it. She'd had a lot of wine and it had left her loose and relaxed and maybe a little daring. It had definitely washed away her earlier warnings and vows to herself about resisting Shane. Plus, she'd spent several hours with him tonight and, wine or no wine, she was so completely infected with his charm, his charisma, with the pure joy of being with him, that she just didn't—couldn't—care about anything but fully indulging herself in that moment with him.

And when he kissed her the second time, there was plenty to fully indulge in.

Somewhere in the split second just before his lips met hers, the kidding disappeared, and when he kissed her this time, he meant it.

His arms wrapped around her and held her in their powerful circle, pulling her against him, one hand reaching to catch her head as he pressed it backward. His mouth opened over hers, urging hers to do the same, to free the way for his tongue to come calling. To test the edges of her teeth. To find her own tongue. To explore and learn and tease and delight all at once.

Maya's arms went around him, too. She flattened her palms to his broad, hard back and followed the expanding rise of it into shoulders so broad she could barely reach them.

And she let her tongue play, too. Met his and matched it. Danced and teased and charmed and cherished, falling deeper and deeper into his kiss with every passing moment.

No, there was no joking in this. In fact, it grew more and more serious. More and more passionate. More and more arousing, lighting sparks inside her that glittered to life. That caught flame in spots that cried out for some attention. For his touch. Maybe even for the feel of his velvety mouth.

Her breasts strained against the confines of her bra. Her nipples tightened and begged not to be ignored. And lower still, regions of her body were coming to life that shouldn't have been.

But for no reason she understood, somewhere in the back of her mind she also began to hear Suzy Teeblat and Marcy Lumbly's words. The scorn in their voices echoed through her brain. And she felt the sting.

She felt it sharply enough to suddenly stop kissing Shane. To suddenly stop letting herself be carried away by him. By wanting him.

"I...need to go in," she said in a voice that made it sound as if she'd just had a rude awakening.

"You don't *need* to."

"Yes, I do," she insisted. "I really do."

"Back to arm's length, huh?" he said with a soft smile and no condemnation at all.

"It's just late and you should get home and Mom will be wondering where I am and—"

"It's okay," he said gently. "Taking our time is a

good thing. At least that's what I keep telling myself," he added with a wry chuckle.

Then he got out of the truck and reached a hand in for her, a hand that held hers the whole way up onto her mother's porch and then turned her to face him again.

"I'm not too sure what's goin' on here, either, Maya. But somethin' is. Somethin' definitely is," he said, holding her eyes with his, searching them as if the answer to whatever it was that was going on could be found there. "I mean to take it slow, but the minute I'm with you… Well, I forget it all and get carried away."

Then he kissed her again—more chastely this time—before he left quickly, as if to escape getting carried away once more.

And even though she knew better, the only thing Maya could think about as she watched him go was that she wished she was still in his arms, still kissing him, and headed for doing a whole lot more.

So much for resisting him no matter what it took, she thought, feeling terribly weak willed.

But with the lingering memory of being in his arms, of his kiss, she also felt more wonderful than she could ever remember feeling before.

Six

The next morning Maya fixed a big Mother's Day breakfast for Margie, then gave herself over to what her mother wanted to spend the holiday doing—peeling wallpaper off the living room wall so she could have the room painted.

They finished shortly before three o'clock in order for Maya to have a quick shower and shampoo, jump into a red camp shirt and a pair of khaki chinos, run a brush through her hair, apply just a hint of blush, mascara and lip gloss, and head for the church to help with the big Mother's Day dinner.

As she crossed the park square she had mixed feelings about the event. On the downside she'd already encountered the night before the worst of her earlier tormentors in Suzy Teeblat and Marcy Lumbly, and she had no desire to meet up with them again. Which was why she usually didn't socialize when she visited her mother and why she wasn't thrilled about participating in this communal dinner, where she could well encounter them again.

On the upside, she didn't think she was likely to find Shane at the dinner, which meant that for the first time since arriving in Elk Creek, she was going to make it through a full day without seeing him or being put through the emotional turmoil that seeing him inspired in her.

At least she tried to tell herself that was the upside. But for some reason it seemed as much like the downside as did the prospect of meeting up with Suzy Teeblat and Marcy Lumbly.

For someone who had always had a clear vision of what she did and didn't want in relationships with men, it wasn't easy going through this confusion. And it was all Shane's fault.

Maya had never known anyone who made her feel all he made her feel—when she was with him and even when she wasn't. She'd never known anyone who could make her feel all that he did as *fast* as he'd made her feel it. And even though she was absolutely convinced it was good to avoid him and all he did to her, she somehow couldn't keep from missing him.

No amount of talking to herself, of warning herself, of reminding herself of all the reasons she should remain aloof and unaffected by him—of all the reasons he was as risky to her as Shag Heller had been to her mother—changed the fact that every ounce of her being wanted to see his great face. To hear his deep voice and feel his powerful arms around her. To press herself up against that long, hard tower of muscle and give herself body and soul over to his unbearably sweet kisses.

"Yeah, you and a gazillion other women," she muttered to herself as she crossed Center Street to the church.

But even knowing the man had a wealth of other women who she felt sure would tempt him beyond endurance sooner or later, even knowing that Shane was quite possibly only dallying with her the same way Shag Heller had dallied with her mother, she still couldn't help wishing there was any chance at all that he would show up at this dinner so she could be with him.

You've got it bad for him, a little voice in the back of her mind said.

And the little voice was right. She did have it bad—really, really bad—for Shane.

Too bad to stay in Elk Creek and tempt fate any more than she already had, she realized suddenly. And in that realization, she also knew that it was time to go back to Cheyenne. To her regular life. To sanity. Because nothing she was doing now to resist Shane was working. Instead she was finding more and more things about him that she liked. She was more and more drawn to him. She was getting in deeper and deeper, just the way her mother had with Shag. And if she was honest with herself, she had to admit that she was also coming to care deeply for Shane.

And she just couldn't let that happen. Or at least she couldn't let it go any further than it had.

So, since her work here was basically finished, she came to a decision as she neared the outside entrance to the church basement. She would make one last visit to see Buzz the next day, pack her bags and head for home the morning after. And, between the Mother's Day dinner Shane wouldn't have any reason to attend tonight and the last home visit, which she would plan for the middle of the day when he was bound to be out working the ranch, it was possible she could leave town without seeing him again at all.

Which should have been a great relief to her.

But somehow it wasn't.

"Maybe you're just a glutton for punishment," she muttered once more to herself.

Or maybe she was already in over her head. Just the way her mother had been with Shag Heller....

"You came!"

Tallie's voice called from a distance to interrupt her thoughts as Maya passed by the brigade of barbecues being set up outside the church, and went into the basement.

But her eyes barely touched on her old friend before sliding like magnets to the man standing beside Tallie just inside the entrance.

Shane!

Shane was there!

After just hashing through all she'd hashed through on the way there, she saw him standing big as you please, glorious in tight blue jeans and a chambray shirt with the sleeves rolled up, ready to get to work with the rest of them.

And Maya wondered if she was tempting fate or if fate was tempting her.

"Hi," she said weakly, glancing from Shane to Tallie to include them both in her greeting.

He just smiled at her, a smile that washed heat through her, leaving her helpless to his appeal and struggling to concentrate on Tallie as she spoke.

"Kansas told me she'd roped you into this but I didn't think you'd be here. We even had a bet," Tallie said.

"Mom wanted to come tonight so I thought it was only right for me to lend a hand," Maya answered feebly as she tried to take her eyes off Shane.

But she couldn't do that any more than she could ignore how wonderful he looked, so she said, "I didn't expect you to be here. Or did your mother come into town sometime today?"

"Nope. She's in the Bahamas with my father for a combination Mother's Day-Father's Day vacation Ry and I sent them on. But I do this with her in mind on the years we can't get together."

"So this is how it works," Tallie said, diving in to explain what they'd all gathered there to do. "Some of the men do the cooking—hot dogs, hamburgers and chicken out on the barbecues—and the rest of the men and those of us women who aren't mothers take care of things in here. I was just going to help Shane put tablecloths out on all the tables, but since you're here, why don't you do it and I'll come along behind with the place settings."

What could Maya say to that? *No thanks, it would*

*be better if I do something else because Shane is as
infectious to me as a fever?*

So instead she said, "Okay. Sure. Whatever." But
she said it without any enthusiasm.

Tallie didn't seem to notice. She just said, "Great—
then I'll leave you to our guy here," and headed in
the direction of the kitchen.

"Hey there," Shane said in private greeting once
Tallie had gone.

"Hey there yourself," Maya responded, at a loss
for anything better to say.

An image flashed through her mind of getting on a
roller coaster, a roller coaster she seemed incapable of
not riding with this man. She spent every hour she
wasn't with him telling herself why she should stay
away from him, then felt awkward and, at the same
time, incredibly drawn to him when she set eyes on
him, only to have him break down her reserves with
no more than a smile so that she ended up in his arms
as if that were where she was meant to be.

It was exhausting. And frustrating. And happening
again as she stood there looking up into jade eyes that
seemed to be feasting on her as if he were starved for
the sight.

"How's Buzz?" she asked in a hurry when it finally
occurred to her that the two of them were standing
there staring at each other as if they were both in a
trance, and the old man was a safe subject.

"He's fine. Tired out after his shindig last night, but
I kept him off his knee by lettin' him beat me at about

thirty games of gin rummy today, and Ry's stayin' home with him tonight to keep him company in front of the television so he can rest up.''

"Did your cleaning crew come in today and take care of the mess?"

"The crew plus a few extras," he said, sounding disgusted.

"Extras?"

"Three single mothers of the crew." His tone conveyed the purpose of the single-mothers contingent—more women in pursuit of one of the world's most eligible bachelors. "I think I'm gonna have to get married just to get some peace," he added with a wry chuckle.

"Did you two just come to gab or to get a job done around here?" Tallie called from the door to the kitchen, teasing but with a message.

"Looks like we better get busy before the boss fires us," Shane said, bending over slightly as if he were sharing a confidence.

He smelled clean and fresh, and the hint of soap scent beneath his usual aftershave went right to her head. It clouded Maya's thinking for a moment before she got a grip on herself.

"Tablecloths. We're suppose to be doing tablecloths, right?" she said.

"Right."

Shane led the way to a stack of plastic-lined paper coverings on a nearby stand and they got to work.

Not that it seemed like work to Maya as what remained of the afternoon flew by. She and Shane seemed to be designated a team, so most tasks were relegated to them together. But with dinner being a group effort and then a good portion of the townsfolk showing up for the meal itself, they were never alone.

Maya told herself that spending this time with Shane, wasn't getting her in any deeper. But a secret part of her knew that wasn't true. Every time she lost sight of him, she made up an excuse to find him, and only when she was with him did she genuinely enjoy herself, but the small self-delusion of safety made her feel better.

The battalion of mothers who came to eat were treated like queens, even though the food, prepared mainly by men who rarely cooked, was nothing fancy. Margie seemed to relish being waited on for a change, as did Junebug, whose husband and six sons all had a hand in the festivities.

A long succession of toasts were made to the guests of honor by their respective families and by friends when no family was present, making a fast dent in the wine supply. The toasts brought a lot of laughter, a few tears here and there, and made the event special for everyone.

A somewhat smaller group stayed behind to clean up after the guests of honor departed. Maya and Shane were among them, and once again they did most of their chores together, chatting easily about some of the more memorable toasts and the people who had made them. Before Maya knew it, the church basement was back in order, good-nights were said all around, the minister ushered everyone out so he could lock up, and she found herself in the cool evening air, with Shane still by her side.

"It's too early yet to call it a night," he said without preamble. "How 'bout a walk in the park?"

"I don't think I sat down more than five minutes since I got out of bed this morning. Walking home is about all I have left in me," Maya said with a weary laugh.

"Okay. How 'bout we go halfway in—which is on the way to your mother's house—lie on the grass and look at the stars for a while? It'll give you a breather. I even have a blanket in my truck," he added, as if it were an enticement.

"I really should get home," she hedged, even though what he was proposing was tempting. Very tempting.

"Your mom said she was tired and going straight to sleep the minute she got home. No sense in you sittin' there in front of the TV while she snoozes, is there?"

"No," Maya allowed tentatively, running quickly through the why-she-shouldn't-go-along-with-this reasons in her mind and still not paying them much heed.

"Doesn't a little stargazin' sound better than that?"

Much better. And after all, it seemed pretty safe to be right in the middle of town, out in the open. Even if Elk Creek did roll up the sidewalks by eight o'clock on a Sunday night while everyone went home to prepare for the start of a new week.

"I suppose it would be okay," she finally agreed, still tentative because her pulse had already kicked into overdrive at just the prospect of having a little time alone with him, warning her that she was once again venturing into dangerous territory.

But warning or no warning, she didn't budge from that spot as Shane made a dash to his truck where it was parked in the church lot, grabbed the blanket from inside and came back. When he reached her on the return trip, he slipped his arm around her waist as naturally as if it belonged there, and any idea of them as a team, or just co-members of a group, changed into something far more intimate and connected and coupleish. And the fact that his touch worked its usual magic and sent glitters of delight sparkling throughout her bloodstream didn't help matters.

"Come on. I know the perfect place," he said, leading her across the street and up the slight knoll into the park with its sporadic canopy of oak and elm trees.

Victorian benches lined several paths that were lit by Victorian pole lights, and he followed one of the paths in the direction of the central pavilion—an octagonal gazebo big enough to be a bandstand and dance floor under a gabled roof.

He took her near the gazebo, where a break in the trees would allow them a view of the sky, and spread the blanket there. Then he swept an arm outward, motioning for Maya to sit.

It looked altogether too appealing. As appealing as he looked with the moonlight christening his sharp, chiseled features and dancing in his streaked, haphazard hair. And she knew she really shouldn't take the step onto that blanket, that if she did, she was seriously tempting fate.

But somehow she just had to do it. She just had to throw caution to the wind and give in to the urge that was more powerful than she was.

So she did. She stepped onto his blanket and sat primly with her back straight, her legs crossed Indian-fashion and her hands folded in her lap.

It made Shane chuckle as he stretched out beside her, leaning on his elbows. His long, thick legs were crossed at the ankles, leaving the pointed toes of his cowboy boots aimed at the treetops.

He rolled his broad shoulders as if to get a kink out of them and let out a long sigh that said it felt good to relax after all their hours of work. The sight of him—even out of the corner of her eye—did wild things inside Maya that made her want to run her hands over those powerful shoulders and feel them roll beneath her touch.

"Can't do much stargazin' sittin' like that," he said, motioning with his chin at her posture.

She knew she must look silly and stiff and priggish. Not things she wanted to be. Plus, if she sat back a little, maybe she'd do more looking at the sky than at him and be less inclined to flights of sensual fancy.

So she forced herself to ease up a bit by placing her

hands palms down on the blanket behind her and leaning her weight on them to look heavenward.

He chuckled again, low in his throat, as if he knew that was as much as she could concede and that even that was hard-won.

"Tell me what it was like growin' up here—before you were a teenager and all that ugly business with Shag Heller changed things for you," he prompted. "Did you like old Elk Creek then?"

"I like old Elk Creek now," she replied. "I just don't like some of the people in it."

"That's true of any place. But what about as a kid? What was important to little girls growin' up here?"

"What was important?" she repeated with a laugh of her own, not quite sure what he was asking.

"For boys growin' up where I grew up it was important to prove what big men we were. That we weren't afraid of anything. Earnin' our stripes, I guess you could say."

"And how did you earn your stripes?"

"Through some serious rituals," he joked with mock solemnity. "Pokin' a dead skunk with a stick. Runnin' into a cave rumored to have bats. Spendin' the night in the woods tellin' the worst ghost stories we could think of to scare ourselves silly. Tryin' to ride wild horses. Takin' any dare thrown our way. Important things like that—a lot of bluster and bloody noses."

Maya smiled at him, imagining him as a boy, venturing all he'd outlined to prove himself a man. It was hard to picture him not being as confident and comfortable with himself as he was now. But all that bluster and all those bloody noses must have worked, because he was definitely a man. All man. Incredible man…

"What was important to little Maya?" he reiterated, sounding slightly like his grandfather when he called her that.

"I'm afraid it was not too exciting."

"You did a lot of girl things, huh?" he said sympathetically.

"Couldn't be helped. I was a girl."

His agile mouth stretched into a wide grin as he looked at her and gave her the once-over. "Yes, ma'am," he breathed in a sexy sigh of appreciation. "But what was important to you?"

Maya had to think about that. Nothing had seemed important enough to make an indelible impression. All she could come up with was, "I had a pretty happy childhood here. It was a good place to grow up. I did the usual kid stuff—minus poking dead skunks and exploring bat caves or riding wild horses. Bike riding and picnicking and doll playing—but none of it seems what you'd call important. I was close to my mom, though—she was important to me. Especially since my father died before I even knew him and there was just the two of us."

"I can't imagine what it would've been like to only have two people in a family. We were five kids, both parents and my grandparents on my father's side until they passed on, all livin' together. It was always a full house.''

"Was that good or bad?"

"Good, mostly."

"Is that what you want for yourself?" Maya asked.

"Must be. I've got the house set up for everybody to move in if they want to, and Buzz is there to stay, that's for sure. But there are more bathrooms now," he added wryly. "We only had one growin' up, and I'm here to tell you that wasn't enough."

Maya laughed and glanced at him again, enjoying this as much as she'd enjoyed every other time with him, even if this was more laid-back and completely devoid of anything physical. There was a sense of intimacy between them just the same. A strong one. Almost stronger than any physical kind. It felt nice just getting to know him.

Not that there wasn't also a part of her that was itching for him to touch her. Or just hold her hand. But he didn't seem inclined to do that tonight and she certainly wouldn't instigate anything, so she merely looked back to the sky again.

"So what's important to you now?" he asked.

Keeping herself safe from heartache was the first thing to come into her head. And yet so was being there with him.

"My work," she said, spinning away from that last thought.

"And that's it?" Shane asked in disbelief. Or maybe in disapproval, she couldn't be sure.

"My mother is still important. So are my friends," she added.

"What about your future? Have any plans for that?"

"I may eventually move into private practice. Do more therapy than casework."

"And what about your personal life? Do you ever want to marry? Have kids?"

"I'd like to get married, have kids," she said, but she could hear the uncertainty and lack of conviction in her own voice. "What about you?" she countered, before he could pursue it. "You built your house with your existing family in mind, but do you want to get married? Have kids, too?"

"Sure," he answered without hesitation. "You said yourself that Elk Creek is a good place to raise kids."

"If you live a straight-and-narrow life and don't offend any moral sensibilities," she reminded, maybe too stiffly because it made him chuckle again.

"I thought I would live on the straight and narrow and do my best not to offend any moral sensibilities," he repeated as if taking an oath, teasing her.

"It's easier said than done with all those women throwing themselves at you," she pointed out.

"Are you sayin' I don't have any moral fiber?" he challenged, again clearly only kidding around.

She felt his eyes on her and couldn't help glancing at him, sounding much more serious than he did. "I'm saying you're only human."

"Sounds to me like you're sayin' I'm a horn-dog."

His comically wry tone took some of the wind out of her sails and made her laugh yet again. "No, just human."

He held her eyes with his as a small smile quirked one corner of his mouth. "Well, yes, ma'am, I'm that all right," he admitted with an edge of pointed innuendo aimed directly at her, as if she alone tempted him.

Here it comes, she thought, expecting him to reach for her. To pull her to lie so that her body matched the length of his. To wrap his arms around her. To kiss her until she was lost in mindless abandon.

And she was ready for it. Craving it. Wanting it, in spite of everything.

But instead, he just winked at her and sat up. Then he nodded at the gazebo and said, "How 'bout a dance?"

Maya laughed—with a little quake to the sound of it as the hot flash of her expectations was disappointed. "Dance? There's no music."

"I'll hum you a little ditty," he promised. But he didn't wait for her to answer before he reached for her hand, stood and took her with him.

She half thought he was kidding again until he got her up onto the gazebo, swung her into his arms and began to hum as he stepped into a slow country waltz.

No, he wasn't kidding. He was absolutely serious. Intent, even, as he led her in time to the "ditty" he was humming so softly she could barely hear him.

And so Maya went along for the ride, allowing the

remnants of tension to be soothed out of her by the slow movement of their bodies together, relaxing into his arms as he held her with perfect propriety, letting the quiet of his deep voice carry her away as if it were a lullaby.

He held her closer and closer as they went on dancing—so close she had no choice but to lay her cheek against the hard wall of his chest. And when she did, he rested his chin atop her head, tenderly, almost lovingly.

She could feel the warmth of his breath in her hair. She could hear his heart beat a steady, strong rhythm. There seemed to be a spot where her head fit as if it had been carved for her, and the longer they danced, the more their bodies seemed to fuse together, melding soft curves to hard muscle, fitting hill to valley, hollow to crest.

And after a while Maya thought that she could go on like that forever. Forever being led in perfect, graceful, smooth motions to the sound of music Shane created just for them.

Little by little he slowed their dancing until they were barely moving at all, just swaying there in one place. She hardly noticed when he stopped humming, but when she felt him lift his chin from her head, it seemed only natural to raise her face to his, to see what was going on.

Her eyes met his and lingered, only peripherally seeing the return of the small smile that washed his expression just before he lowered his mouth to hers.

The kiss was sweet and gentle. A courting kiss. Well mannered and not presumptuous. At first, anyway. But before long it deepened. Before long his lips parted over hers, urging hers to do the same. Before long his tongue came to say hello, teasing and playing sexy games of cat and mouse, which she played along with the whole way.

Before long they weren't dancing at all but were somehow against the railing that circled the gazebo, against one of the spindled posts that helped brace Maya's back as their kisses grew more insistent, more hungry.

And there in Shane's arms she had the sense of achieving what she'd been wanting with every fiber of her being since leaving his arms the night before. Which made all her vows to herself, all her talking to herself, all her purported determination to avoid him nothing but a smoke screen, she thought.

Yet she couldn't deny herself. She just couldn't. She had to taste the delicacies his expert mouth offered, she had to fill her hands with the feel of his broad back widening as she wended her way up to those expansive shoulders she'd itched to explore earlier. She had to caress his thick neck and slip her fingers into his hair. She had to slide her palms to his pectorals, to his biceps. She had to arch her back so that breasts that were alive with a desperate wanting could press against him, so that her hips could meet his and she could know by the hard ridge that met her there that she wasn't alone in her need for this.

Their kisses turned deep and urgent. Shane's hands began an exploration of their own, pulling her shirt free of her waistband and rising up underneath it. Skin to skin for the first time sent a shiver through her and forced a tiny groan from her throat, erupting in a driving need for more—for all of her to be naked against all of him.

But for the moment she had to content herself with only his hands working wonders on her back, no matter how strongly she wished he would work those same wonders on her front.

Maybe the second arch of her spine telegraphed that message to him. Or maybe he merely read her mind, but as one hand stayed to brace her, the other traveled a delightfully torturous path to her side, up her rib cage and finally—*finally*—to her breast.

She cursed the bra that kept him from reaching bare flesh, from reaching the nipple that cried out for his touch. But he didn't leave her suffering for more than a few minutes before he slipped adept fingers inside the lacy cup, easing it downward.

And if the initial feel of his hand against her bare back had been wonderful, this was near to ecstasy as the yearning orb fitted into his palm with the same perfection as every other part of their bodies.

It felt so incredible another groan escaped Maya's throat—this one low and raspy as Shane teased, tormented, kneaded, circled and deliciously pinched her nipple into a hard knot of desire.

A hard knot of desire echoed in other regions of her

body and cried out for more. More of his hands on every inch of her. More of his mouth on every inch of her. More of everything...

Except that instead of more, she suddenly got less.

Shane tore his mouth from hers, slid his hand from her breast and let his head drop back as if he were on fire and needed deep pulls of air to quench it.

"Not here," he said in a husky, ragged voice, as if she'd suggested something. "I want you more than I want to breathe, but not here in the middle of the town square."

Until that moment Maya had lost sight of where they were, and of everything but the needs he aroused in her.

But there they were, all right—out in the open. In the middle of town. Up on the grandstand that all outdoor events centered around.

"Let's go somewhere else. Somewhere private," he said.

But Maya had had time enough to come to her senses by then. To remember what she should have been remembering all along. And to know that no matter how much she wanted Shane, wanted him to make love to her, she couldn't go through with it at that moment. Not there or anywhere else. Not when she felt as vulnerable to him as she did at that moment—vulnerable to all he represented to her.

"No, I don't think so," she whispered.

He held her against him again, breathing hot gusts into her hair, cradling her head to his chest as if he couldn't let her go. But he didn't argue the point. He just stayed that way for a long while. Maybe until he had himself under some kind of control, because eventually she felt the tautness passion had put in his big body ease.

"You're in my blood, Maya," he said then.

"Like poison?" she asked, attempting to make a joke but only managing it halfheartedly.

"I don't know. Are you aimin' to annihilate me?" he asked with too much solemnity in his tone not to sound as if he were actually serious—maybe even worried—about it.

"I'm not aiming for anything," she said softly.

"Maybe cupid is," he said in an obvious attempt to lighten things between them.

"I need to get home," Maya informed him, knowing if she stayed in his arms any longer she wasn't going to be able to contain the yearning for fulfillment of all he'd awakened in her.

"I'll walk you," he said, loosening his hold on her.

"No," she answered in a hurry, too afraid of what would happen between them if they didn't say goodnight right then and there. Plus, she needed the time alone and the cool night air to regain her bearings before she stepped foot in her mother's house. "I'd rather go alone. Think of it as a cold shower," she added with a little laugh.

"Cold or not, if we do it together—"

"Right. Together we're combustible."

He kissed her once more, softly, sweetly, and yet

still with a simmering, smoldering passion held at bay just below the surface. Then he opened his arms as if setting free a bird.

"If you don't get out of here now, I'm not lettin' you go at all," he warned.

A part of her wanted to stay just to make him prove it. But a stronger part finally took hold and Maya stepped away from him. She didn't go far, though. She stayed feasting on the sight of him for a moment.

And then she muttered, "Good night," and turned to nearly run from the gazebo and across the park toward her mother's house. Taking with her even more confusion about what was happening between the two of them. And a deep, deep craving to ignore it all and just follow her heart. Back into his arms....

But following her heart was what her mother had done. Not what Maya ever allowed herself to do.

Seven

"I just came to tell you I'm giving this living arrangement my stamp of approval," Maya said to Buzz late the next afternoon, once they'd dispensed with the amenities.

She and the old man were in the sitting room portion of his quarters—he was on the couch and she was on one of the overstuffed chairs. Buzz had on his bathrobe—loosely belted over an undershirt and baggy boxer shorts—his cowboy boots and his raggedy Stetson. Apparently now that the walker allowed him mobility, Junebug was losing the battle to keep the disreputable hat and boots away from him.

Maya felt overdressed in her blue twill slacks, white cotton blouse and sandals.

"What's 'at mean—yer givin' us the stamp of approval?" Buzz asked.

"It means I'm going back to Cheyenne on tomorrow's train and I'll write up a report saying you're comfortable, welcome and well taken care of, so there's no reason you can't stay here rather than going to a nursing home."

"Then what?" he asked impatiently, as if that weren't the answer he'd been looking for.

"Then I'll check in periodically by phone with you and with Tallie—I've already met with her today to arrange it—and you'll both give me progress reports. But essentially what it means is that Social Services will stay out of your business unless you need us."

"Shane know yer leavin'?" Buzz demanded suspiciously.

"No. I thought you could tell him." That way she wouldn't have to be tempted by him again before she left town.

She'd had a sleepless night after fleeing the park square the previous evening. A sleepless night in which she'd struggled mightily to force herself not to slip out of her bed and into Shane's. But having won the war, this morning she had renewed her vow not to see him again, to leave Elk Creek before it was too late and before whatever was happening between them went too far.

The trouble was, being there in his house, having the sense of him all around her was making that vow difficult to keep.

"I think you better talk to 'im," the old man decreed.

"It's really not necessary—"

"Sure 'tis. I know 'tis."

"You can tell him what I've just told you. I don't have to bother him."

"Ain't been a bother to 'im yet, havin' you anywheres 'round. You can't go slinkin' outta town without tellin' 'im yer goin'."

"I don't think I'd be slinking."

"G'wan out to the barn—that's where he's at by now."

"The weather station is predicting a bad storm and I'd like to get back to Mom's before—"

"Ain't no storm can compare to the storm you'll cause if'n you don't go out to that barn right now an' tell 'im what yer doin'. G'wan."

"My business here is with you."

"G'wan," the old man insisted.

Maya debated with herself. She considered standing her ground, flat out refusing rather than doing all this hedging. She considered lying, saying she'd seek out Shane, then just leaving for home instead.

But the longer she was in Shane's home, the longer she marinated in the sense of him all around her. The more Buzz pushed her, the stronger grew the urge to feast on just one last glimpse of Shane. To have just one last moment with him....

"G'wan," Buzz repeated when she didn't move from the chair.

"Well, maybe just for a minute," she heard herself say before she realized she was going to concede. But now that she had, she reasoned that a few moments of saying goodbye wouldn't be too dangerous and it might even put some kind of closure to things.

As she stood, she said, "I'll probably just go straight out to my car once I've talked to Shane, so you take care of yourself, Buzz. And cooperate with Junebug and Tallie for me, will you?"

"Humph! Too many hens," he grumbled, but not seriously. Then he raised a cheek to her, pointed to it with a gnarled index finger and said, "Give an old man a little peck."

She laughed and did just that before abandoning him to the television program he'd been watching when she came in.

Junebug wasn't in the kitchen when Maya got there so she crossed the spotlessly clean enclave, went through the French doors and out to the patio without ceremony.

A storm was definitely brewing, she thought as she peered up at the sky. Heavy, dark clouds hung low and ominous. Lower and more ominous than they'd been all day.

It was good incentive to keep this encounter with Shane to a minimum, she told herself. To get in, say a few quick words and get out before the rain hit.

Because even if she couldn't keep her vow not to see him at all today, she was still sticking to the rest of her decision to get out of Elk Creek as soon as possible. She had to—that was all there was to it. Things between her and Shane were rushing forward with a will of their own—like a runaway train—and the only way she knew to stop them, to be completely safe, was to remove herself from the tracks.

"Just get in and get out," she told herself. "And leave him to the legion of other women who want him." That reminder helped to steel her and she headed for the huge, state-of-the-art barn as an ear-splitting crack of thunder sounded overhead.

It was good to think about the bare-breasted woman on the train as she went. About the exquisite woman in the café. About the woman who had literally broken into Shane's home to get to him. About the woman in stiletto heels and the women in town who were all over him—Suzy Teeblat and Marcy Lumbly among them. If she was going to give in to seeing him this one last time, she knew she needed something to help her at least keep her distance. And what could be better than remembering one of the major reasons he was too great a risk to her?

But somehow, as she left the perimeter of the patio and spotted Shane coming out the door that led to the paddock alongside the barn, the fact that there were so many temptations to him, so many other women for her to compete with, so many other women who wanted him, faded into the distant recesses of her mind, and all she could think about was how much *she* wanted him.

He was carrying a sack of feed on each shoulder, headed away from her toward a lean-to, with a slightly bowlegged walk that had just a hint of swagger to it even beneath what had to have been considerable weight. Nearing the paddock fence, she studied the line of his broad back as it narrowed to his waist. Her gaze slipped to his incredible, jean-encased derriere, all the way down long, powerful legs, and she drank in the sight of him, trying to brand every inch of him into her memory.

He tossed both feed sacks to the ground and split open one of them to empty it into a bin covered by the lean-to. As he did, he glanced over his shoulder as if he'd heard her approach, and in that instant it seemed to Maya that time stood still and everything around them receded into the distance. As if the moment her eyes met his, they somehow stepped out of reality into a world all their own.

His eyebrows arched as he registered that she was coming toward him. Then his whole face lit up, easing into a smile, then a grin that showed her how glad he was to see her, too, melting the starch right out of her.

"Hey there, cute stuff. Where'd you come from?" he asked as he shook out the last of the feed and tossed the sack into a rack above the bin.

Maya finally made it to the railed paddock fence and he stepped up to face her from the other side of it.

"I came from the house. I was with Buzz," she answered, knowing she'd made it sound like an ordinary visit and not the last of them. But even as she told herself to say a quick goodbye to Shane and leave, something kept her from doing it.

"I was just thinkin' about you," he said. "Not that that's unusual these days. Or nights," he added with a wickedly teasing tone. "Seems like I can't get you out of my head nohow."

"Maybe you need a good brainwashing," she joked.

"Sometimes it gets pretty dirty, all right," he agreed, going along with her play on words.

Another clap of thunder struck, making Maya jump with surprise.

Shane looked up at the overcast sky and shook his head. "Sounds like we're in for it," he said. "Maybe we better hightail it up to the house before it hits."

"I didn't mean to interrupt your work," she said with a nod toward the bin and the lean-to, silently urging herself to tell him she was leaving town and then go before they ever got back to the house together. But still she just couldn't quite do it.

"You aren't interruptin' anything," he assured her. "I have one more sack of feed to put in that bin and I'm finished up for the day. Stay put and I'll be right with you," he ordered.

Maya watched as he went back to where he'd been before and split open the second feed sack. Thigh muscles swelled against the denim of his jeans when he hoisted the grain to let it pour into the bin. His hair was unruly and marked all the way around with a crease where his hat had been. His lean, sharp jaw and shallow cheeks were shadowed with beard. There were salt stains under the arms of his faded gray work shirt, and he looked like any hard-driven ranch hand who'd just put in long hours of backbreaking toil.

Again, not the image Maya suspected other women had of him. Yet she still found him heart-stoppingly handsome and so appealing that nothing could puncture her pure appreciation of him. And somehow telling him what she'd gone out there to tell him was suddenly overshadowed by thoughts of having this one last time with him.

He tossed the second empty sack into the rack with the first and wiped his hands against the seat of his jeans. Maya's gaze followed and her mouth went dry at the sight. She wasn't sure if she wanted it be her hands on his rear end or his hands on hers. Probably both.

He crossed the paddock once again, only this time instead of stopping at the railing, he hopped over it in one lithe, graceful motion just as another earsplitting clap of thunder sounded.

Shane shot a look skyward again. "I think we better get inside," he suggested, placing a hand at the small of her back as they turned toward the house.

They'd made it about halfway when lightning flashed, immediately followed by a boom of thunder so loud the ground shook. As if something had ripped in the sky, just that quick rain poured down in a torrent so hard it was as if buckets of water were being thrown down upon them.

Shane grabbed Maya's hand and they made a run for it, reaching the shelter of the covered patio within minutes. But it still wasn't quick enough not to be soaked to the skin.

Maya blinked water out of her eyes and smoothed her hair back from her face, then glanced down at herself to find her white blouse nothing more than a transparent film that revealed her lacy bra beneath it.

She tried pulling the soaked, clinging fabric away from her skin, but it had little effect and she finally settled for crossing her arms over her breasts as camouflage.

Shane shook like a wet dog, ran both his hands over his face to dry it and then looked at Maya rather than at his own sodden, muscle-cleaving shirt.

"Whoo-ee! After all those threats today, when this weather finally decided to hit, it didn't fool around."

And maybe it was a sign telling her to get out of there the way she was supposed to, Maya thought.

"I think I better go home before it gets any worse."

"No, ma'am," he said in a way that let her know he wouldn't even consider the possibility.

"It'll be all right. I shouldn't stay anyway. I just—"

He cut her off. "This storm is bad enough already and I'm not lettin' you go anywhere in it."

"You're not *letting* me?" she repeated with a disbelieving little laugh at his high-handedness.

"That's right—I'm not lettin' you."

"You're keeping me captive?"

"Call it what you like, but you'd need to go through me to get out of here in this, and I can tell you, you're no match for me."

He was curiously serious and Maya found it odd enough to test. "I've driven in rain before," she informed him, as if she fully intended to do it again now.

Shane pointed a thumb to the slight scar that altered

his left eyebrow. "Me, too," he answered as omi-
nously as the clouds that darkened the sky so much it
looked as if dusk had descended around them.

Then he caught her hand again and led her not into
the kitchen but to the wraparound porch that connected
to the patio, heading to the bedroom wing opposite of
where Buzz's rooms were.

"We don't want to track water into Junebug's
kitchen or she'll have our heads on a platter," Shane
explained as he made his way past several doors to
the one closest to the front. He opened it as if it were
a separate entity from the rest of the house and waited
for Maya to go in ahead of him.

Oh, good, she thought. *I wasn't supposed to even
see him today, and here I am, slipping into his bedroom from the outside entrance like a thief in the
night.*

"Come on. Let's get you out of those wet clothes,"
he said, compounding the sense that they were doing
something clandestine. Not that she seemed to have
much choice. Or that she was sure she'd have chosen
otherwise if she had.

But when she stepped inside, she realized it wasn't
his bedroom he'd led her to but the sitting room that
adjoined it, and like Buzz's sitting room, it wasn't
much different from going into a self-contained, luxury apartment.

"You know, you could turn this place into a dude
ranch and rent these rooms out as suites," she ob-

served as she glanced around the space, which was as opulent as the rest of the house.

"In case I ever hit hard times?" he asked, sounding amused by the thought.

"You never know," she allowed.

He just laughed. Then he finally looked down at himself, assessing the damage. "I need a shower with a little soap. How 'bout I get you something to change into while I do that?"

One more quick look at her own see-through blouse was all it took to convince Maya to agree.

Shane went through a connecting door and brought back a towel, a crisply folded chambray shirt and a pair of jeans.

"Try these," he suggested as he set them on the back of the leather sofa that faced the fireplace. Then he held out a hand—palm up—and said, "Now I'll take your keys," as if demanding them from a drunk driver.

"I beg your pardon."

"I don't trust you not to run out of here when my back's turned, and I told you I'm not lettin' you drive in this. So I'll take your car keys."

He was serious about that, too.

It piqued her curiosity all the more as she wondered why this was so important to him.

With one arm still over her nearly exposed breasts, she fished her car keys out of her trouser pocket and held them poised over his palm.

"I'll give them to you on one condition."

"Name it."

"That you tell me what the big thing is with driving in the rain."

"Deal," he agreed, snatching the keys. "As soon as I don't stink like a sweaty wet dog anymore," he promised. Then he pretended to get a bad whiff of himself, made a face and turned on his heels to go into the bedroom portion of the suite.

He hadn't pulled the adjoining door completely closed. It was only slightly ajar but Maya's thoughts wafted right through the crack he'd left. She pictured him stripping down on the other side of that door, crossing to the bathroom, getting into the shower and letting a steamy spray of water christen his naked body until it glistened.

And what she wanted to do more than she wanted to breathe was follow him into that bathroom. To see for herself what she was only imagining. To get into that steamy spray with him…

But she didn't have the courage.

So she went to the door and silently closed it the rest of the way, as if that would wipe out the fantasy. Or at least bolster her resistance to it.

Then another shiver struck her and helped bring her back to her senses. The sudden chill reminded her that she needed to attend to herself before he returned and wondered why she was still standing in the middle of the room moony-eyed.

So that was where she focused her frustrated energies. She kicked off her sandals and removed her slacks first. The hems of her pant legs were sopping from sloshing through the instant puddles that had formed outside, but the rest of the pants weren't damp enough to have soaked through to her bikini underwear, leaving them dry enough to keep on. But once she'd peeled away her blouse, she found her bra equally as soggy and already beginning to chafe, so both the blouse and the bra had to go the way of the slacks and sandals.

She made quick work of putting on Shane's chambray shirt over just her panties, glad the shirt couldn't be seen through. It was very large, though, as it would need to be to fit Shane. The tails reached her knees, and she had to fold the sleeves back half a dozen times just to free her hands and wrists.

But it was soft against her skin and had a faint, fresh smell she associated with Shane. She couldn't resist burying her nose in the upturned collar to take a few deep breaths of the scent, which was probably nothing more than the detergent Junebug used to wash the clothes. But it didn't matter. To Maya it was Shane's smell and it made her head go light just having it wrapped around her.

When she'd breathed in enough of his scent to temporarily satisfy her—and fearing he might come back and catch her with her nose in his shirt—she raised her chin above the collar and did a fast scan of the room in search of a mirror or something she could use as one.

The best she could come up with was a silver ice

bucket on the wet bar in one corner. Using it, she discovered her hair was drenched. But without a brush or comb to get out any tangles, she was careful to blot it dry with the towel before she used her fingers to fluff it away from her head. Since she ordinarily wore it long and straight anyway, it didn't end up as unsightly as she'd worried it might.

Her face wasn't too much the worse for wear, either. The slight dusting of blush she'd put on before leaving her mother's house was gone, but the mascara she'd used was waterproof, which meant it was still in place and hadn't smudged—for which she was grateful.

Content that she didn't look bad enough to send anyone shrieking into the night, she deserted the ice bucket and went to the sofa to retrieve the jeans Shane had also brought. As she pulled them on she tried not to imagine what they usually encased. But it was no easy task, and the very idea that they had cupped that perfect derriere of his…and more…sent yet another shiver through her, this one having nothing whatsoever to do with a chill.

The jeans were not as easy to conform to her size as the shirt had been. There wasn't an ounce of fat on Shane, but even so he was a big man, and there was no way his jeans would fit her. She had to pull the long legs up in several increments, and even once they were buttoned and zipped they practically fell right back around her ankles when she let go of them. Without a belt or tie of any kind to help hold them in place, she decided she'd better hurry up and set her clothes out to dry so she could be sitting by the time Shane came back.

She used the towel again, this time to wring out as much water as she could from her bra so she could hide it discreetly underneath the driest part of her slacks when she laid them out. Next came her blouse, which she smoothed on the shag carpet beside the pants.

She was still on the floor on her hands and knees, struggling with the tangle of the overlarge jeans, when Shane called through the closed door, "Are you decent?"

Worried that he might come in without waiting for much of an answer, she tried to make her way to the couch in a hurry. But her feet caught in the long legs of the jeans and she nearly fell into the coffee table. As it was, there was a loud thud when she crumpled to the floor.

"Are you all right in there?" Shane asked.

"I'm fine," she answered, sounding a little frazzled. But to prove she really did have everything under control, she opted for staying on the floor, sitting in front of the sofa as if by design rather than because of an inability to fight her way to her feet while still keeping her pants on.

"Can I come in?" he asked again.

"Sure," she said as if there were no problem, and hoping she didn't look as silly as she felt.

He opened the door and stepped inside, dressed in another pair of jeans and a pale green shirt, which he'd left open and untucked to flap around his hips as he towel-dried his hair.

He'd shaved to erase the day's growth of beard and his handsome face looked fresh scrubbed. Between that and the strip of well-muscled chest and flat belly that peeked out at her, Maya's stomach did a flip-flop with just one look at him.

"The clothes work all right for you?" he asked, surveying the results of her changed attire.

"Sure," she repeated. "As long as I don't stand up, because these jeans won't stand up with me."

He smiled. "You could take 'em off. From the looks of that shirt, it covers as much as a short skirt."

It did. But the thought of what it *didn't* cover made her shy. "That's okay. We aren't going for a jog or anything, anyway. You were going to tell me about why driving in a rainstorm makes you nervous," she reminded him pointedly.

He glanced out the big picture window next to the stone fireplace, smiled devilishly and nodded at the torrential rain still falling beyond the veranda's overhang. "I may have to readjust my thinkin' about rainstorms since this one got you trapped here with me."

His hair seemed to be as dry as it was going to get, so he tossed the towel aside and ran a hand through it to smooth it back. On anyone else that haphazard grooming might have ended up making him look a mess. On Shane it only made him look tousled and oh-so-sexy.

But rather than give her the explanation she was

fishing for, he crossed to where she had her clothes laid out. "Can these go into the dryer?"

"No. They'll shrink. But I think they'll dry out pretty fast there."

"I have a better idea. I'll lay them out in the bathroom under the heat light."

"No, that's okay—" she started to say to keep him from discovering her hidden bra. But he was quicker, and before the words came out of her mouth he had the lacy undergarment held up in the air and a devilish grin on his face to go with it. A grin that made him look like an ornery boy enjoying the mischief he'd wrought.

He studied the bra for a moment in what looked like appreciation, then said a simple, "I'll take good care of this," and left the room with everything in hand.

Maya closed her eyes and sighed, trying to extinguish her embarrassment before he got back and remembering much too vividly that it wasn't the first time he'd had an intimate encounter with her underwear.

But it was a toss-up as to whether she was more embarrassed or more stirred up inside with wishing the second encounter had been more like the first....

Shane still hadn't buttoned his shirt or tucked it in when he returned moments later. And he didn't bother with it then, either. He just joined her on the floor—pushing the coffee table in front of the couch out of the way so he could sit close beside her.

"All taken care of," he assured her as he settled in.

Maya's back was braced against the front of the couch but Shane angled more in her direction, with one leg down on the floor, the other bent at the knee to allow a perch for one arm. His other arm stretched along the seat cushions, his hand close enough to the back of her neck for her to feel the heat of it without him actually touching her.

"Come on. Spill it. Tell me the rainstorm story," she ordered to get her mind off the realization that he was so near she could smell the heady scent of his aftershave.

But still he didn't launch into an explanation. Instead he took her keys from his pocket and gave them an underhand throw to land on the coffee table.

Then he replaced his forearm to his upraised knee and finally said, "I was drivin' home from town in a storm like this four years ago. Couldn't see ten feet in front of me but figured it wasn't anything to worry about. Not that much traffic on these country roads, know 'em like the back of my hand, not far from town to home—all the things we think about familiar territory. Then, from what looked like out of nowhere and drivin' right down the middle of the road, goin' too fast, was another car. I was goin' faster than I should have been, too. I swerved, he swerved, but it was too late by the time we saw each other and we hit head-on."

Maya grimaced and gave in to the reflexive urge to

trace the scar in his eyebrow with her index finger. "I wondered where you got that."

"I hit the windshield far over to the left so the metal window frame cut a straight shot—"

"Into your eye?" she asked before he could say it, horrified by the thought that hadn't occurred to her before.

He nodded solemnly. "Didn't know for a good long while if I'd lose the eye altogether. Or at least my vision in it."

"No wonder you're wary of storms. Were you alone in the car?"

"I was in an old truck without air bags, but yeah, it was just me."

"And the other driver?"

"He did some hospital time, too. But we were both lucky to survive."

Maya nodded. "Lucky is right."

"In more ways than you know."

"You lived to tell the story, you didn't lose your eye or your sight, and all you ended up with is a little crease in your eyebrow—how much luckier than that were you?"

"It cost me the woman I was about to marry."

Maya frowned. "And that was lucky?" she asked.

"I was engaged to a woman named Penny Baker at the time. Thought I'd finally found somebody who wasn't just the kind of party girl Ry and I had had our fill of—"

"Party girl?" Maya interrupted for clarification.

It was Shane's turn to grimace as he talked about years of attracting women not unlike the ones Maya had had the misfortune of crossing paths with lately.

"Don't get me wrong," he said. "For a long time that was okay with us. We did plenty of playin'. Plenty. But after a while it got old. The kind of women we were dealin' with, why they wanted us in the first place, started to be more of a turnoff than a turn-on. We both decided we ought to make some changes in whom we chose to keep company with. It just never occurred to either of us how hard that change might be to make."

"But you thought you'd made it in this Penny person," Maya guessed.

"Mmm. Thought so."

"But you were wrong."

"Oh boy, was I wrong! She was as shallow as the rest. Maybe even worse. She took one look at me in that hospital bed, asked me what kind of shape my face was in underneath all the bandages and didn't want anything to do with me if there was even a chance that I might end up scarred."

Maya's own eyebrows rose at that. "She wasn't just glad you were alive?"

"I don't think that crossed her mind. Any more than she could understand why I was a hell of a lot more worried about losing my eye and my sight than I was about any damn scar."

"She didn't care about whether or not you came out of it being able to see?"

"She cared about how I was going to look and that's it," he reiterated disgustedly. "I might have only had the use of one eye at the time, but it opened right up to her. Even *before* she tried to seduce Ry in my hospital room when she thought I was sleepin'."

"Oh, no," Maya groaned sympathetically. "I'm sorry."

"Don't be. I was glad to find out the truth about her before it was too late."

"It still must have rocked you. Especially when you were laid low physically and afraid of having permanent damage. What a rotten time to have to deal with the woman you loved not being who—or what—you thought she was." Maya gave in to a second urge to touch him. She ran her finger along his brow and across the scar, wanting to ease even just the memory of the pain and disillusionment he'd let her be privy to.

"Women," she said in gentle, mock exasperation to lighten the tension that lingered in the air around them. "They're only after one thing."

Her joke made him smile as he took her wrist and lowered her hand so he could kiss the same finger that had just smoothed his brow before he let go.

"Some of 'em *are* only after one—or two—things," he agreed wryly.

"I'm sure glad that can't be said of men," she pointed out facetiously.

"Oh, it's true of some men, too," he allowed, as if it were a revelation.

"But not you. Not now that you've been enlightened to the deeper meaning of the whole man-woman thing," she teased.

"Don't go givin' me a hard time here, cute stuff. Remember I have your underwear in my bathroom, and if you ever want it back, you better behave yourself."

"Did you learn blackmail during your years of debauchery?"

He chuckled and shook his head, then looked at her, arching that quirky eyebrow but speaking with a more serious note in his voice. "What I want from you I want given freely, not because you've been blackmailed into it."

"And what would it be that you want from me?" she asked, but the joking had ebbed from her voice as she looked into those jade green eyes of his. He strummed something inside her with the warm feel of his big body mere inches away and the sight of his handsome face.

"Everything," he said quietly, after what seemed like a solemn consideration of how to answer her question. "I want everything from you. Everything *of* you."

Maya's gaze did a slow roll from his eyes down his long, ridged nose, to his high-peaked, roller-coaster mouth, which offered such delights, to that off-center indentation in his chin, and back again.

And all the while she couldn't help thinking that she was leaving town the next day. That this really was her last time with Shane. Her last chance to follow her heart just once. Just once....

She raised her thumb to his brow for a third pass over his scar—this one light and sensual—letting her fingertips continue the course along the side of his face as his eyes held hers.

Just this once...

She raised her chin slightly, as if challenging him to kiss her.

But he didn't take the challenge immediately. Instead he closed his hand around the nape of her neck, doing a soft, sexy massage that reached up into her now dry hair to cup her head before he came slowly, slowly nearer, barely touching his lips to hers in that first meeting.

Not that it mattered, because just that much was enough to set off sparks in her bloodstream. To once again wash through her the sense that something more was at work around them, between them, connecting them. Something powerful. Something too intangible to put a name to. Something amazing.

It was just the way it had been earlier, when she'd seen him at the barn. The rest of the world receded and she had the sense that the two of them were in a world of their own when they were together. A world where she belonged to him and he to her....

Shane's lips parted and Maya followed his lead, welcoming his tongue as it came to play games she was now familiar with. She teased and toyed, chased and caught as much as he did, relishing the dance.

Shane used the hand at the back of her head to pull
her deeper into the kiss and Maya did him one better—
she eased the rest of herself closer, too, and reached
a hand to his chest.

She hadn't for a moment forgotten that it was exposed between the open sides of his shirt, and her palm
was itching to be pressed flat to the bare skin, as
smooth as silk, stretched over hard muscle.

Her own nipples kerneled and ached to be free of
the shirt she wore, to replace her hand on his chest
and find their niche there.

But if she couldn't have that, she could at least raise
her other hand to his biceps and savor the feel of that,
too, wondering if other parts of him were as thick and
hard....

His tongue stopped playing games and began a languid exploration as mouths opened wide and hungry.
Still one hand cradled her head, but the other slid up
from her waist all the way to the side of her neck.
Featherlight fingers rubbed circles of comfort. Of
temptation. Of arousal. Of promise.

Circles that dipped inside the collar of her shirt and
found her collarbone, tracing it to the hollow of her
throat, where his thumb nestled perfectly until it trailed
from there to the first button that barred his path to
better things.

He slipped the button from its hole with studied
precision, almost too leisurely for Maya's taste. The
anticipation of feeling his hands on her breasts again
was a terrible yearning to be soothed.

But there was no hurry to him as he gave the same attention to the next button and the next, all the way to the end.

Even then his hand didn't slide inside the way she thought it would—the way she wanted it to. Instead he wrapped his arm around her and pulled her up against him, her bare breasts to his naked chest, just as she'd longed for moments before the desire for the touch of his hands had infused her.

Nice. It was very, very nice. But by then she needed so much more.

Still holding her, Shane eased her backward onto the floor, going with her to lie partly beside her, partly on top of her.

He slipped his hand into the shirt, but only to her shoulder. She couldn't be sure if he was teasing her by delaying what she wanted so much or just moving slowly to ease her into it. Either way, she wished he'd speed things up.

"If you don't touch me soon I'm going to go crazy," she heard her own voice whisper in a brief moment between kisses.

Shane chuckled low in his throat, as if he knew exactly what he was doing and was enjoying this bit of tender torture the way she'd glimpsed him enjoying his mischief with her bra.

He forcefully recaptured her mouth with his open one, still taking his sweet time working her shoulder with the same strokes her breasts cried out for.

And then he began a slow descent in that direction,

reaching one straining mound with the wonders of that big, powerful hand.

Maybe he'd known what would happen when the two areas of flesh connected, and had thought to put it off, to drag out those delicious warm-ups as long as he could, because when his hand closed over her breast, it was as if both Maya and Shane caught fire. Nothing from then on was slow or leisurely or studied. It was all urgent and hungry, demanding and intense, as if they'd both been starved for the feast that was now suddenly right there for the taking.

Hands searched and explored—his and hers—mounting glorious desire with every caress, every teasing pinch, every kneading, squeezing touch.

Maya rid him of his shirt altogether so she could have free rein to glide her palms up bulging biceps and pectorals to the mounds and deep crevices of his back, to his waist, and lower still to cup that magnificent derriere she'd only laid eyes on before this moment.

Shane worked his magic at her breasts—first one, then the other—before tearing his mouth from hers to do even more incredible things with it. Sucking a sensitive orb deeply into the warm velvet darkness, he allowed his tongue to follow the full circle of her nipple, flicking the pebbled crest and tightening a cord inside her that brought her back off the floor and awakened the spot between her legs to a moist desire. The pleasure was so strong she thought she might lose her mind if he didn't fill the raging need there soon.

She reached unabashedly for the buttons of his fly, fumbling slightly but opening them all, feeling the burgeoning of his manhood on the backs of her fingers as she did. Yearning uncontrollably to touch him, to drive him as wild as he was driving her, she forgot all inhibitions and found that hot, hard proof that he wanted her as much as she wanted him, reveling in the feel of the power and strength her hand enclosed.

Shane moaned in what almost sounded like agony and rolled away from her, shedding his jeans in a split second, as if he couldn't endure wearing them another moment longer. Then he reached for the legs of the jeans she wore and—without bothering to unzip them—yanked them off in one fast swipe. Her bikini panties met a similar fate and then he came back to her, the full magnificence of his naked body lying atop hers as his hands each found a breast and his mouth caught hers once more.

But not for long. Blessedly, not for long, before he pushed himself up enough to nudge her knees apart and find his place nestled between her thighs.

Maya's back arched and she was unable even to breathe, she wanted him so much.

He found his home, slipping inside her smoothly, joining their bodies, peg into groove, flawlessly.

And then he started to move inside her, pulsing at first, then building steadily in speed and intensity, until Maya lost herself in mind-numbing pleasure that grew greater and greater with each deep plunge he took into the recesses of her body, her soul.

She clung to his back, matching him rise and fall for as long as she could. And then she just held on, letting him take her all the way through passion's tempest, racing together to a climax that burst upon her— inside her—at the same moment it erupted from him, turning them both into rigid pillars of pure, potent ecstasy that melded them into one, that held them poised in time and space, in white-hot blinding bliss.

And then Maya breathed. Her first breath, it seemed, in a while, as little by little she descended from the peak. She could feel her heart beating in sync with Shane's, each breath as heavy as his. They clung to each other as if nothing could ever separate them.

Shane laid his face alongside hers and those hot gusts of air singed her ear. "I think I'm fallin'," he said ever so softly.

In love? Was that what he meant?

She couldn't be sure. And she was afraid to ask. Afraid of admitting that she might be falling in love with him, too. Afraid that *in love* might not have been what he'd meant.

So she didn't say anything at all, but just tightened herself around him where they were still one and tried not to think about anything but the contentment of being there, like that, with him.

Then he slid out of her and stood, coming back again to lift her into his arms and carry her into the bedroom with a possessiveness that washed away all her fears. He laid her gently on the bed and took his place next to her, pulling her into his arms and flinging one side of the bed's quilt over them.

And within that cocoon of splendor, enfolded in Shane's embrace, her cheek pillowed in the shallow spot just in front of his shoulder, his chin resting on her head, Maya didn't fight the sleep that beckoned.

She just couldn't. Not when everything felt so good. So wonderful. So absolutely, unquestionably right.

Too right to let reality tamper with it just yet....

Eight

Wrapped in Shane's arms as that evening turned into night, Maya lost all sense of time, all sense of everything but Shane and wanting him, Shane and the feelings for him that suddenly ran free and frolicked in her heart.

After sleeping for a while, she awakened to darkness and the soft caress of strong hands on her bare back. The deep, quiet, passion-raspy rumble of his voice teased her, tempting her, luring her into a second round of lovemaking even sweeter and more perfect than the first.

Sated yet again, they drifted into another exhausted slumber, naked body against naked body, arms possessively keeping hold of each other and legs entwined as if they'd been spending blissful hours like that forever and were accustomed to the mesh and melding of every nook and cranny, of not being sure where he left off and she began.

When Shane woke her the next time, Maya felt as if she were floating on a cloud of pure comfort and was only willing to emerge from the dreams that went with it because the promise of yet a third turn at the pleasures he gifted her with was something she couldn't resist.

But the pleasures he had in mind weren't quite the same as those she was looking forward to when she rubbed her cheek in a small circle against his chest and muttered a lazy, "Hmm?"

"If I don't have somethin' to eat soon, they're gonna have to carry me out of here on a stretcher. I'll be too weak to walk."

"Is that a complaint?" she joked in a voice that was low and languid and more sensual than she'd ever heard come from herself before.

"No, ma'am. It's a statement of fact—I need some refuelin' and then I have every intention of takin' a few more laps around the track."

"I beg your pardon." She pretended affront at his metaphor.

He kissed the top of her head and chuckled a hot gust of air into her hair. "You know what I mean," he said in a tone sexy enough to charm away any offense.

"Here's what I think," he went on. "How 'bout I sneak into the kitchen—it's after ten, so Junebug's long gone and nobody'll be in there askin' questions— and I'll rustle us up a picnic supper to eat right here in bed?"

If he was determined that they feast on food instead of each other, then a picnic in bed definitely had more appeal than the thought of her padding around outside his two private rooms and encountering Ry or Buzz. And now that he'd brought up the subject of food she realized she was pretty hungry.

"Want to take my order?" she conceded, innuendo in her tone.

"I'll surprise you," he countered cockily, as if he knew just how to please her. But then, he *did* know how to please her in every other way they'd explored tonight.

Shane gave her a squeeze and kissed her head once more, then slipped out of bed.

Only moonlight filled the room, but as Maya rolled onto her back—careful to keep the sheet over her— she could see just well enough to make it worth the effort.

She watched as Shane crossed to the dresser near the open bathroom door. He was a breathtaking sight of male magnificence gilded in moon glow, and she felt appetites for far more than a picnic supper rumbling inside her.

"Don't be long," she whispered, making him throw her a sly smile over one broad shoulder as he took out a pair of fresh jeans, pulled them on and then went barefoot from the room.

For a moment after he'd gone, Maya lounged in the warm downiness of his bed, picturing him again as she'd just seen him—a hard-muscled rival for any Greek god—and she could hardly wait for him to slide back under the covers with her, to once again have the opportunity to smooth her hands over every inch of that sleek body of his.

Then her thoughts turned to other things—using the bathroom, making sure she wasn't too much of a fright to look at and putting on the shirt he'd loaned her. For modesty's sake. And so he could take it off her again.

That last possibility was intriguing enough to set her into motion. She turned on the lamp on the nightstand and made quick work of getting out of bed, going into the sitting area to grab up the chambray shirt she'd had on earlier and then light-footing it back through the bedroom to the bathroom.

Her clothes were dry on the floor so she picked them up and draped them over the towel bar, having no thought whatsoever of putting them on and cutting short what she'd entered into tonight with Shane— having no thought whatsoever of anything but the moment in time she was indulging in.

Once she'd availed herself of the facilities, used Shane's brush to get the snarls out of her hair and judged herself presentable, she left the bathroom—intent on heading back to bed for their picnic.

But as she passed by the bureau from which he'd only moments before taken clean jeans, something caught her eye. She moved closer to see if it was what she thought it was, fighting off a sudden chill that had nothing to do with temperature.

The top of the dresser was littered with personal things. There was an oversize silver belt buckle that looked to be an award of some kind for the best bull of show at a Texas rodeo dated two years ago. There was an old set of spurs mounted to an oak base set in one corner and draped with a discarded string tie. Shane's key ring and wallet were near one edge. A button that was probably waiting for Junebug to sew it back on looked as if it had been tossed there when it had come loose from a shirt. And cuff links and a gold ring were held in a crystal dish.

Maya's attention was held by what was propped up against that crystal dish. There, right out in the open for anyone to see, was the very distinctive platinum business card the woman in the café had left for Shane. And making matters worse, stuck to it was a slip of paper with a phone number and a Denver address written on it in Shane's hand.

Maya couldn't help studying the display as a voice in her head shrieked, *He kept her card....*

The card of the classy, beautiful woman Maya had thought must be a model. A New York model—although it seemed clear now that the other woman wasn't as far away as New York. She was in Denver. No doubt at the address on the paper attached to the card.

In her mind's eye, Maya replayed the events of that day in her mother's restaurant, seeing Shane pick up the card off the counter at the café. Seeing him put it into his pocket rather than throw it away. Seeing him act as if he weren't interested in the other woman, as if he wanted to elude her.

But he'd kept the card.

And even then Maya had wondered if it was for later reference.

Had he called her? she couldn't help wondering. Had he dialed the number on the card and talked to Miss Carla Carter—the name that burned its way into Maya's brain as she stared at it engraved on the face of the thin metal plate. Had he talked to her, flirted with her, just the way he flirted with Maya? Had he made plans to get together with her and taken down her address and another phone number where she could be reached?

It didn't take much to convince Maya that he had.

I'm an idiot, she thought as that chill turned into a cold blast of reality. The reality that Shane wasn't serious about her. Or at least not any more serious about her than Shag Heller had been about her mother.

And why should he be? He was one of the world's most eligible bachelors. He was one of the world's richest ranchers. He was great-looking. He had a body to die for. He might have tired of party girls, but there were still plenty of other women available for him to pick and choose from like succulent grapes on a vine.

And I'm just one of those grapes.

Just the way her mother had been for Shag Heller.

Idiot! How had she lost sight of that? How had she forgotten it even for one night?

She'd let herself get drawn in, that's how. Drawn in by Shane's charisma, his handsomeness, his undeniable appeal.

But now she'd had a wake-up call in the form of a platinum business card and she knew she had to get out of there. She had to get away from him, away from the feelings she had for him. Feelings that had come unleashed in these last few hours.

She had to get away from the allure she just wasn't strong enough to resist if she so much as looked into his eyes.

She had to go where she could be safe. Sane. Rational. Reasonable. Where she had any chance at all of fighting his pull on her. And she had to do it before she ended up like her mother. Before she got caught in the tender trap of men like Shane and Shag Heller and wasted her whole life trying to compete with women she couldn't compete with, putting her heart at risk, hoping and praying that if ever Shane did get serious, she would be the one he chose.

She rushed to the bathroom again, threw off his shirt and pulled on her own clothes as fast as she could, driven to get out of there without having to come face-to-face with him.

The coast was clear when she'd finished and she half ran across the bedroom into the sitting area, snatched up her keys from the coffee table, jammed her feet into her sandals and tried not to think about what had gone on there on that floor in front of the couch to set this evening in motion.

Or how much she'd liked it.

And then she slipped out the same door they'd come in, onto the wraparound porch at the side of the house, and made a dead run for her car—in the rain that was still falling to mingle with the tears that had started somewhere along the way.

* * *

The last thing Shane expected when he carried the tray full of food into his bedroom was to find it vacant.

"Maya?"

He set down the tray and poked his head into the open bathroom door. Then, when he found that as empty as his bedroom, he tried the sitting area.

But she was nowhere around.

Confused, he went in search of her, not understanding why she'd leave the bedroom but still hoping to come across her looking in on Buzz as he slept or having used another bathroom or searching for who knew what—a book, a pen, a piece of paper, maybe just a view of her car.

But he didn't come across her anywhere at all. And when he looked out one of the windows in the front of the house, he discovered her car was gone.

"She ran out of here a few minutes ago like a rabbit."

Ry's voice came from behind him. Shane turned, spotting his brother sitting in the formal living room, a cattleman's magazine open on the coffee table in front of him.

"Snuck out on you, did she?" Ry asked.

"Appears so."

Ry shook his head in sympathy. "Wouldn't've taken her for one of those."

Shane knew what his brother was referring to as "one of those." He meant one of the many fickle women they'd both encountered too often in their wild days. Women who up and took off at the drop of a hat for any reason—or no reason at all. Mainly just because they'd had their fill and felt like it, because they only thought of themselves, because even the simple courtesy of saying goodbye was more than they bothered with. Because they were fly-by-nights.

"Doesn't seem like Maya," Shane said to defend her, but it came out too weakly as he began to wonder himself.

"Buzz says she came over today to say goodbye. Says she's givin' us her stamp of approval and is goin' back to Cheyenne on tomorrow's train."

That hit Shane like a punch in the gut.

Apparently Ry saw it because he said, "She didn't tell you."

"No."

"Think this was her last-night-in-town fling?"

Shane didn't want to think that but it was looking more and more like a possibility. And it raised his hackles the way it always did when he felt he might have been used. But still there was a part of him that said Maya wouldn't do that. That something else must be going on here.

"She looked pretty unhappy from what I could see through the window when I heard her car start up," Ry offered. "Maybe you did or said somethin' wrong."

"She was happy as a clam when I left her."

"Maybe puritan guilt set in while you were gone."

"Maybe." That actually seemed more likely than the thought that she'd just be using him for a fling. But even it didn't ring any bells with him.

"Maybe you ought to go after her. Find out what's up," Ry suggested.

Shane had been thinking the same thing and that was all the encouragement he needed. By God, the least he deserved was an explanation.

"Take it easy in the rain," Ry called after him as he left the living room.

Shane just waved. There was too much on his mind to do much else.

In the bedroom once again he yanked on socks and boots, then a shirt, all the while replaying his final moments with Maya. She'd told him to hurry back, he recalled, and for the life of him, he couldn't remember anything that even hinted at the kind of coyness that might indicate she hadn't meant it, that she was planning to slip out while he was gone.

But it wouldn't be the first time he'd misjudged a woman.

He grabbed his keys from the dresser and retraced his steps to the kitchen to go out the back door, ignoring the rain that pelted him as he went to the garage and got into his truck, all the while asking himself if it was possible that Maya wasn't what she seemed to be. If she was just one of those shallow women he knew from experience to avoid.

And despite the part of him that had trouble believing it, he still couldn't help worrying that she was.

But why was he so worried about it? he asked himself as he drove away from the house. Why should it matter if she was one of those women? It wasn't as if they were engaged—as he'd been to Penny when he found out she wasn't the person he thought she was. It wasn't as if he had any kind of commitment with Maya, or even any strong ties. If she was just a here-and-gone woman, then so be it. Life would go on the same as before—only with one more lesson to make him wary of whom he hooked up with.

But none of that changed the way he felt. He felt rotten. As rotten as he had when he'd been confronted with the truth about Penny. Why was that? he asked himself.

But deep down he knew why.

Sure he'd been with Penny for longer than he'd been with Maya. He and Penny had had plans for the future—something he and Maya didn't share. But the one thing that was the same was that he'd loved Penny.

And he loved Maya.

In the throes of passion with her it had struck him that he might be falling in love with her. But now he realized he wasn't only *falling* in love with her—he was *in* love with her.

"Great time to figure *that* out," he muttered to himself, making a careful turn onto the main road that led to town.

What if he'd fallen in love with another shallow woman? Just the thought made him cringe. It made him disgusted with himself.

But as he considered it, he also realized that he still couldn't buy into it. Nothing he knew about Maya said she was shallow. As far as he could tell, she wasn't obsessed with her looks. He'd never seen her primping or preening. Another woman would have dived for her makeup kit after coming in out of the rain earlier. But not Maya.

She was a good daughter and had even put aside her own reluctance to meet up with people she didn't like—people who gave her grief—in order to give her mother a day off work, to accompany her mother to Buzz's welcome home party and to do the Mother's Day dinner at the church. That didn't speak of the kind of selfish, self-centered, self-important women Shane had met up with before.

And what about the day he'd come home dirty,

grimy, stinking of horse—at his worst—and found her there? Or even earlier today when they'd met up outside? She hadn't balked either time. She hadn't so much as wrinkled her nose. He'd known plenty of women who would have complained, women who'd wanted him picture-perfect at all times because the way he looked was so damn important to them. But not Maya.

So what the hell was going on with her?

Why hadn't she told him she was leaving town tomorrow? Why had she hightailed it out of his room when his back was turned? And if Ry was right and she'd been upset, what had upset her?

Nothing made any sense.

Except his feelings for her, he thought as he hit town and headed for Margie Wilson's street. But what was he going to do about these feelings once he got there? he asked himself.

He knew what he wished he could do. He wished he'd come to the realization of his love for her while he'd been in the kitchen at home, then carried the tray of food into the bedroom and found Maya waiting for him in bed. He wished he'd been able to crawl under the covers with her, pull her into his arms and tell her how he felt.

He wished they could have gone on from there.

But instead, here he was, pulling up in front of her mother's house, wearing his heart on his sleeve and not knowing what in blue blazes had happened to make her run out on him like that.

"Well, find out," he ordered himself. Maybe it wouldn't be anything as bad as it looked. And then maybe they could still go on from there....

Maya was glad her mother hadn't waited up for her. Glad to come into the sleeping house without having to answer questions. Glad to go into her old familiar bedroom, throw off her damp clothes and pull on her big, comfy terry-cloth bathrobe, cinching it around her waist like a firm embrace.

She'd fought to stop crying on the way home, and now she struggled to maintain her victory. She hated to cry. It only made her feel worse and it didn't change anything. Things were what they were and that was all there was to it.

She towel-dried her hair for the second time that evening and ran her own brush through it. That was when she heard a truck pull up out front.

Her hand stopped in midair, the brush paused in its last stroke and she thought, *Oh, no, don't let that be Shane....*

Because she didn't know how strong she could be if she had to face him.

But when the sound of the truck's door opening and closing echoed through the silence of late night in the small town, she knew it was him, that he'd followed her. And she knew that strong was exactly what she needed to be. Strong enough to protect herself from the potency of his appeal. From all her own feelings for him and what they urged her to overlook.

When the knock came on the front door, she drew herself up, straightened her shoulders and took a deep breath, forcing herself to think of her mother. Of the life Margie had lived—too many nights spent alone in her bed, wondering what other woman Shag Heller was with.

And that wasn't what Maya wanted for herself.

She made it to the door on the next series of more insistent knocks. She opened it and at the same moment drew herself up, lifted her chin and told herself she could do this. She could get through it. That she'd be better off as soon as Shane knew that what was between them had gone as far as it ever could.

She wavered slightly when she saw him, dressed in the tight jeans she'd watched him pull on over his wonderfully naked rear end only a short time before, a shirt he hadn't bothered to tuck in and the ever present cowboy boots. His hair was damp and only finger-combed, and his rugged face was tight with a confused frown that made him no less breathtakingly handsome.

He didn't wait for her to let him in but yanked open the screen and stepped over the threshold before he said, ''Where the hell did you go?''

Nothing like cutting to the chase.

''Home,'' she said simply, as if it weren't obvious.

"But why?" he demanded, frustration ringing in his voice.

"This just isn't going to work out," she informed him as she moved into her mother's living room, which was some distance from her mother's bedroom, so Margie wouldn't be awakened.

"Why isn't it going to work out?" Shane asked, following her into the dim glow of the one lamp lit in front of the picture window. "Things were going great and I turn around and you're gone. Why? What happened? Talk to me!"

Maya shrugged as if it were unimportant. "We had some fun but that's all there was to it. That's all there ever could be to it—and it isn't what I want."

He stared at her as if he couldn't believe what he was hearing. They weren't standing far apart, but still Maya had the sense that a deep chasm had formed between them, separating them by miles.

After a moment in which he seemed to be deciding whether or not to accept her declaration, he said, "That's a load of bull. Tell me what's really going on."

"Look," she said a little more agitatedly. "I'm sorry if I wounded your pride or something by leaving the way I did. But it just occurred to me that we aren't on the same level and you're not what I want."

"Uh-huh. We aren't on the same level," he repeated, as if it were the most ridiculous thing he'd ever heard. "And what is it you want?"

"I want a plain, simple guy who doesn't have the world at his feet. A guy who can be...content with me."

"And between the time you asked me to hurry back to bed and now, you decided I wasn't that guy."

She shrugged her confirmation of that.

"How did you come to that decision?"

If he could cut to the chase, so could she.

"I saw it, Shane."

"Saw what?"

"That woman's business card. The fancy metal one that model—or whatever she was—gave you in Mom's café the other day. I saw that and the address you had written down along with it."

"So?" he asked, sounding totally confused.

"Don't get me wrong. You're a single man—one of the world's most eligible bachelors. You're rich. You can have anything and everything you want. But I won't compete with a legion of women willing to pull up their shirts on trains or climb in your window at night or track you down to offer you whatever it might be they have to give. I don't want to wonder and worry about who you're with if you aren't with me. I watched Mom do it and I'm not interested, so I thought it was just better to call it a day with you."

"You saw that card on my dresser—"

"And the address and other phone number."

"And from that you're leapin' to all this?"

"It wasn't much of a leap. It was more like a reminder of what I knew before but had lost sight of for a while."

"The address and phone number are for a print shop in Denver that sells those cards. Ry and I thought they'd be a good business card for McDermot Beef so I did some calling around and found the place where we can order them. It didn't have anything to do with the woman who left the card."

That took some of the wind out of her sails.

"You can call the number right now," he went on. "There's probably an answering machine with a message that'll let you hear it for yourself."

Was he bluffing? Maya wondered. If he was, he was good at it. Great at it. Or maybe he wasn't bluffing at all and he was just telling the truth.

But did it really matter? she asked herself. Because even if it was true, even if he hadn't called the woman, that still didn't change the fact he could have. Or the fact that that woman and a gaggle more were waiting around every corner for him. And that Maya would never know which one of them would tempt him away.

She just shook her head. "It doesn't make any difference."

"Why is that?"

"She was only one of many, Shane. They throw themselves at you and sooner or later there will be some that you're willing to catch. I don't blame you. It's one of the perks of looking the way you do, of having all you have, of being you. But I don't want a man like that.''

He gave a harsh, mirthless chuckle. ''I've had too many women fall in love with the packaging and ignore what's inside the box. Now, here you are, shyin' away from the packagin'. Thinkin' there isn't enough substance inside to bypass other women—no matter how many or what they're offerin'—and settle for just one. There's something wrong with that.''

''There's something wrong with being what you'd 'settle for.''' She used his own words as a weapon to prove her point.

''I'm not talkin' about settlin' *for*. I'm talkin' about settlin' *down*. That's not something I could do with a woman like the one on the train or any of the rest who've been chasin' after me. They don't want me—at least not the me I really am. They want the conquest. They want what they see on the outside. They want the bank account. They don't know what I'm about as a person and they don't give a damn.''

He sighed a disgusted sigh, glanced over his shoulder as if he needed a moment to control his own anger and then looked back at her with narrowed eyes and an expression that seemed disappointed in her.

''On the other hand,'' he continued, ''if you really knew the man I am, you'd know I don't give a damn about playin' around with a bunch of women or huntin' for some fantasy female. So maybe you never looked past the packagin', either.''

That stung.

"What I think is that you're only human and eventually there will be a woman—or two or three—who are just too much to resist," she explained.

"What *I* think is that a man with any kind of character at all, who makes a commitment to one woman, can keep from strayin' because he values what he has with that one woman."

"There's no commitment here."

"And if I want there to be?"

That stopped Maya cold. Did he mean it? Did this go along with his earlier comment that he was *falling?*

But even if it did, even if he genuinely wanted to make some kind of commitment, even if the falling he'd referred to was falling in love, did that really change things?

She didn't think so.

Because even if he meant what he was saying now, that still wouldn't alter the fact that the world and all the women in it were his for the taking. Just the way it had been for Shag Heller. It didn't alter the fact that she'd never know—with so much available to him— if and when he opted to sample some of it. And she just couldn't live with that uncertainty.

Besides, he wasn't declaring his love for her. He wasn't begging her to marry him. He was talking in *ifs,* in generalities. Just the way Shag Heller had done to keep her mother on the line for so many years without ever really keeping the ambiguous promises he made.

Maya shook her head in denial. "This just isn't what I want."

"Why not?"

"It just isn't. Plain and simple—that's what I want in a man and that's not what you've ever been, what you'll ever be."

"You just don't think you're good enough, do you?" he said, as if those searching green eyes of his had lit on the truth buried deep inside her. "That comment you made about our not bein' on the same level—that's what that meant, wasn't it? All those years of bein' put down by the Suzy Teeblats and Marcy Lumblys of this town when you were young and vulnerable stuck with you. And even now you don't see that you don't have to compete with anybody because you've already got 'em all beat. You're just lettin' a bunch of old insecurities get the better of you. The better of us."

"I just know how I want to live my life and how I don't."

"I think you're just too damn scared to live it at all."

She raised her chin at him. It was the most rebuttal she could muster.

"So you're gonna get on that train tomorrow and run the hell away like you ran the hell away tonight?" he challenged.

"How'd you know—"

"Buzz told Ry, Ry told me. Might've been nice if you'd told me yourself. Before. I might not have wanted to be your last fling before leavin'."

The second sting.

"It wasn't like that," she defended herself feebly.

"What was it like, then?"

"You know."

He raised that single quirky eyebrow with the scar in it rather than letting her off the hook.

"I was going to tell you," she insisted. "I went out to the barn to tell you. But you know what it's been like between us. When we're together...things get... out of hand...carried away. You said it yourself."

"We're combustible all right—just the way *you* said we are. And you're willin' to walk out on that?"

"I can't let it cloud my judgment." *And cost me my whole life the way it cost my mother hers....*

"What if I asked you to stay?"

She shook her head once more.

"What if I told you I'm in love with you?"

Sweet talk. It had done her mother in and Maya had a sudden flash of understanding because she wanted so desperately to believe that Shane loved her. To let herself be convinced that his loving her would make everything work out. But she knew better and she just shook her head yet again.

"What if I told you I think you love me and if you leave you'll be stealin' a good thing for us both?"

Again, she shook her head stubbornly.

"So that's it?" he asked, his voice raised louder than it had been.

"That's it," she confirmed quietly but steadfastly.

"You're bein' a damn fool, Maya Wilson."

She couldn't even shake her head at that because maybe she was being a damn fool. She didn't know. She only knew she just couldn't let go and do anything else. It felt too much like letting go of her lifeline and allowing herself to be swept away in the rush of a raging river.

He studied her for a long moment, as if the pure power of his gaze could change her mind.

But when she didn't budge, he said, "Fine. If that's how you want it. You know where to find me if you change your mind."

Maya didn't say anything at all. She just stood her ground. Shane took another turn at shaking his head, then spun on his heels and left.

And as Maya watched him go, she wondered why she didn't feel relieved. And safe. And good about having finally resisted all she'd been trying—and failing—to resist since the first time she'd set eyes on him.

But she didn't feel any of those things. None at all. Instead she felt as if her heart had been ripped out of her body and flung on the floor.

And that was when the tears started to flow again.

Nine

"Maybe we should have a cup of tea."

Maya jumped a foot at the sound of her mother's voice coming from behind her as she stood at the picture window, staring out at the rain.

Shane was long gone, but no matter how hard she tried to feel good about it or how much she told herself it was for the best, she still felt unutterably awful.

But she didn't want her mother to be burdened with that.

"I'm sorry if I woke you," she said without turning from the window.

"I was awake when you came in. And I heard that whole thing just now with Shane," Margie added, warning her daughter not to waste time denying anything that was going on. "Let's have tea and talk."

Maya heard rather than saw her mother head for the kitchen. It gave her a few minutes to fight back the tears, to go into the bathroom and splash some cold water on her face.

When she joined Margie at the round walnut table in the warm pink kitchen, there were already two cups of tea waiting and her mother was sitting on one of the barrel-backed chairs, stirring sugar into hers.

"You're making a mistake," Margie told her without preamble as Maya sat down. "I want to know what's been going on inside your head all these years to bring you to the conclusions you've come to about Shane."

Maya didn't jump into that explanation. She couldn't. There were things she and her mother just didn't talk about. Had never talked about. And Margie's relationship with Shag Heller was at the core of it all.

But Margie wouldn't let her get away with any more of the silence, and finally—choosing her words very carefully so as not to hurt her mother—Maya confided that she'd always been afraid of giving her heart to any man after what Shag had done to Margie.

"And is Shane right about you thinking you're not good enough to hold on to him when other women are after him?"

Maya didn't answer readily. "It isn't as if I don't think I'm good enough," she said. "I just don't want to have to compete forever for the man I love."

"So you do love him. I thought so."

Do I? Maya asked herself. But it wasn't as if she didn't know. She did know. She loved him. She loved him in a way she'd never felt for anyone in her life. It just didn't change anything.

Margie shook her head sadly at Maya, an expression of regret shining through the nightly cold cream. "That's my fault—your not feeling like you're on the same level with a lot of other people," she said, ignoring Maya's denial. "I let us get treated that way. I ignored the town talk to have Shag, and now I see that a girl growing up in the middle of that kind of scorn would get scarred by it. I always hoped Shag would make an honest woman of me and that would redeem me and make the talk stop, get us back some respect."

But of course that had never happened.

"I don't think it *scarred* me," Maya protested.

"I think it did. So does Shane—that's what he meant by your letting old insecurities get the best of you. That's why you think you can't compete with other women."

"It isn't that I think I *can't*. I just don't want to."

"Because you figure you won't win. That somebody else will end up with him the way somebody else ended up with Shag."

"This isn't only about me," Maya pointed out to change the subject, because her mother was hitting uncomfortably close to home. "It's about Shane, too."

"And him being like Shag—rich, powerful, able to have anything and anyone he wants instead of being a plain, simple man," Margie finished for her, repeating some of Maya's own words. "But you're looking at the wrong things, Maya. Money and power aren't what make a man good or not so good. It's the man himself. And how he thinks of you. Shag always thought of me as his backdoor romance. It wasn't me who thought I wasn't good enough for him to marry, it was him. I tried to pretend that wasn't true, but that's how he saw me."

There was so much self-disgust in her mother's tone that it made Maya ache for her and she didn't know what to say.

But Margie went on before she could come up with anything.

"Listening to Shane tonight, it didn't seem to me like that's how he sees you. He's a better man than Shag was and that's what you should be taking into consideration. Even just fishing around tonight the way he was about loving you, about you loving him, about wanting a commitment was more than I could ever get out of Shag because he liked stringing me along, liked being in control of everything between us. He liked that I danced to his tune, always letting me hope that sooner or later he'd actually marry me if I did. And he liked sneaking around behind my back with other women, too. Just for the fun of it, to prove his prowess. It didn't matter how much it hurt me."

Margie's disgust was for Shag Heller now, and it was the first time Maya had heard her mother speak ill of him. Not even when he'd ended their relationship and Margie had had her breakdown had she said anything against him.

"I'm not proud of any of this," she continued. "I'm not proud of having been so weak…or so desperately in love with a man like that. But I was, and I'm telling you now because none of what Shag Heller *was* sounds like the man Shane *is*."

No, it didn't. But still Maya had some difficulty

escaping the fear that had followed her through so many years.

"But Shane was only posing some what-ifs about loving me, about making a commitment," she pointed out.

"Because you were cutting him off before he could get past those what-ifs. Because you weren't giving him an inch. If you had…well, I doubt you'd be here right now feeling miserable."

"I don't know…" Maya said dubiously.

"Take it from somebody who was dangled for a dozen years—what you heard from Shane tonight wasn't anything like what Shag did to me. Stop comparing the two of them—the only way they're alike is in the bank account department. Stop worrying that you're going to end up like me and go after him. Go after what you want," Margie ordered.

Then she stood and took her cup to the sink before she headed for the hallway that led back to her bedroom.

But before she got there she paused, and in a quiet, heartfelt voice, she said, "Don't let what I did ruin this for you, honey. Don't let my mistakes and my weaknesses keep you from being happy. From being with Shane. I couldn't live with it."

Then Margie left Maya to the tea she hadn't so much as sipped. She stayed staring into the amber liquid, her mother's words echoing in her mind.

Was Shane a better man than Shag Heller had

been? she asked herself. But she didn't have to ponder it long to know the answer. *Of course he was.*

Shane didn't have any of Shag's mean streak, any of Shag's need to play games or maintain some kind of power trip—or to prove his prowess. But there were more differences than that.

Shane had integrity and loyalty. He was down-to-earth. Devoted and committed to his grandfather. There was nothing pretentious or arrogant about him. He really was a better man. A man of character. A man of character who just might value her and what they had together enough not to stray—as he'd said.

Was she letting old insecurities get the best of her, the way he'd accused? The way her mother believed?

It suddenly seemed like it to Maya. Why else would she feel as if any strange woman who came hunting for Shane were such a threat? He hadn't looked twice at any of them. She'd only imagined that whole scenario over the business card. And he'd told her himself how unappealing he'd found the kind of women who'd been chasing him—even before they chased him the way they did now.

Besides, some of the very things she loved about him—the fact that to just look at him or listen to him made it impossible to tell how wealthy or successful or powerful he was—should have convinced her he wasn't the playboy type or anything like Shag Heller—and that he wasn't interested in a harem of fancy, flashy women. That deep down he really was the plain, simple man she wanted.

But he hadn't told her outright that he loved her. He hadn't proposed, a little voice in the back of her mind reminded. He hadn't said anything definite about a future together.

And he wouldn't. Not now that she'd rejected him, ended their relationship and left him thinking nothing could breach the barrier she'd erected between them.

You know where to find me....

She heard again his parting words and realized the ball was in her court. If she didn't go to him, if she didn't open up to him, tell him she loved him, they'd never have a chance for anything more. They wouldn't have any future at all.

So go to him, she urged herself.

But what if all he wanted was more of the dalliance they'd had since she'd arrived in Elk Creek? What if he hadn't been serious about their making a commitment? What if his idea of a commitment wasn't marriage but an arrangement like the one her mother had had with Shag?

The reemergence of that fear was still immobilizing.

But if that's all he wanted, she reasoned, then she still had the option of getting on tomorrow's train and going back to Cheyenne. She didn't have to accept what he offered the way her mother had accepted it from Shag.

But if she didn't go to Shane, she'd never know for sure. She'd have lost the opportunity for a future with him without ever having tried to have one.

And she knew she couldn't live with that. She

couldn't live never knowing if they might have been able to have more. If they might have been able to have a life together. A lifetime.

"I'm going out," she called in the direction of her mother's room as she headed for her own to get dressed again.

"Good," was all Margie said, sounding relieved and as if she didn't for a moment doubt Maya was doing the right thing.

All Maya could do was hope that was true....

The rain had stopped by the time Maya threw on a pair of jeans and a navy blue T-shirt, dabbed on a little blush and mascara, ran a brush through her hair and charged out of her mother's house. The air was crisp and damp and sent a shiver through her as she got behind the wheel of Margie's car.

Or maybe it wasn't so much the cool temperature as it was the potential outcome of her errand. Good and bad. But either way, she ignored the shiver and drove faster than Elk Creek's thirty mile an hour speed limit allowed in her eagerness to get to the McDermot ranch.

Don't let it be too late. Don't let it be too late, she chanted silently the whole time, keeping her fingers crossed that she wasn't wrong about Shane, that he wasn't the same kind of man Shag Heller had been, that he would want more for them than Shag Heller had wanted with her mother.

There were no lights shining from the front of the

McDermot house when she got there. And since she didn't relish letting Ry or Buzz in on what she was about to do, she decided before she even turned off the engine that she'd retrace the path she'd taken earlier and go straight to Shane's private rooms.

It seemed like a good enough plan.

There was only one problem.

Her mother's car was not new and Maya had locked all four doors from the main control on the driver's side door after she'd gotten in—force of habit from living in the city. But when she tried to unlock them the same way, she discovered that they wouldn't move.

She poked the button repeatedly and it made the sound it usually did, but the locks just didn't respond.

Muttering impatiently to herself, she tried pulling up the manual lock, but apparently the entire mechanism was jammed because that wouldn't budge, either. Not on her door or the passenger door or either of the doors in back.

After climbing all over the car to try each one, she slid into the driver's seat again and closed her eyes in frustration. This was not a complication she needed right now.

Thinking that the locks might work if she started the engine, she tried that, too. But to no avail. She was still stuck in the vehicle.

Unless she climbed out the window.

So, with the engine running—and praying the power

windows would work even if the locks wouldn't—she pushed the control button for that.

Luckily it responded and down went her window. It was no easy task climbing out of it once she'd turned off the motor again, though. Her first attempt was to pull herself up to sit on the window's edge. The trouble was, once she got there and was sitting, staring over the top of the car, she couldn't seem to go anywhere else. The window wasn't big enough for her to swing her legs through. She couldn't get a good enough grip on the roof to pull herself the rest of the way upward or get a foothold on the edge to climb out that way.

And then, to make matters worse, she accidentally hit the horn in one of her attempts, sending a beep into the stillness of the night that sounded much louder than usual.

Deciding that the only way she was going to get completely out was face first, she slid back inside, maneuvered a difficult turn and did a conservative nose-dive out the window.

She managed to catch herself—palms down on the gravel-covered ground—and then tried getting the rest of her body out with a careful crab-walk on her hands. That was when she came nose to toes with a big pair of cowboy boots.

With her rear end up in the air, her legs hooked over the car window's edge and her arms supporting her weight, she craned a look up long, jean-clad legs to a slightly bulging zipper, a flat belly exposed between an open shirtfront and the face of the man who she hoped had enough respect for her to want her in a more dignified way than her mother had been wanted.

She didn't think the pose helped.

"If I remember right," Shane said in that deep voice above her, "I grab your ankles and we call this the wheelbarrow race."

The grabbing-her-ankles part seemed like a good idea so he could ease her lower half from the inside of the car. Otherwise she was a little afraid she was going to end up with a faceful of gravel.

"Call it whatever you want, but I'd really like to get out of here."

"Mmm-hmm," he muttered. But rather than taking hold of her ankles, he grasped her under the arms and lifted her up and out at once, setting her feet on the ground.

It left them face-to-face, close enough to kiss and staring into each other's eyes.

For a moment Maya thought everything was going to be all right. That they were just going to pick up where they'd left off and act as if the scene in her mother's living room had never happened. It caused her spirits to rise considerably.

But then he let her go and stepped back as if he wanted distance between them, not helping her resolve one iota.

She wiped her wet palms over the legs of her jeans,

then tugged her T-shirt down, trying to reclaim some aplomb. "Thank you."

"Sometimes it helps to open the door to get out," he informed her.

"The locks stuck. Old car," she said, glancing at him from the greater distance.

His hair was mussed, as if he'd drawn agitated fingers through it numerous times, and he wasn't smiling. He was just watching her. Warily. And what Maya hated most was that she suddenly felt like just another woman making a clumsy attempt to chase after him.

"Can we talk?" she asked quietly, needing to screw up her courage enough just to stay there.

Shane held his arm out toward the house and waited for her to go ahead of him.

"Would you mind if we went into your sitting room so Ry and Buzz don't have to know I'm here?"

"Whatever you like," he said neutrally.

Maya headed for the house, remembering Shane's accusation that maybe she hadn't looked beyond the surface of him any more than the shallow women he avoided. She couldn't help wondering if that had soured his feelings for her. It seemed like a possibility with the way things were between them at that moment, and she had second thoughts about the whole thing.

But when she considered not going through with it, she knew she couldn't back out now. Couldn't leave Elk Creek without giving this a try, even if it did cost her some pride—or at least what was left of it after the car incident.

Neither of them said anything as they rounded the house. Once they'd reached Shane's side door, he opened it for her and let her precede him there, too.

The sitting room portion of his suite was just as she'd left it—the coffee table askew, freeing the way for what had begun earlier in the evening. And for the second time that night, Maya couldn't look at that spot without having too many things stirred up inside her.

She turned her back to that part of the room, facing Shane as he followed her inside and stopped just far enough to close the door after them.

He crossed his arms over his chest where it peeked through the shirt he must have been about to shed, tipped more weight onto one hip than the other, and said, "You wanted to talk," as if it were a challenge.

"I just had a long chat with my mother," she told him, deciding there was no reason to beat around the bush. "She heard everything we said tonight and helped me to see a few things more clearly. Mainly that you were right about me and I was wrong about you."

"How so?"

Maya explained it all to him, letting him know he'd hit the nail on the head about her insecurities, even though she hadn't wanted to admit it—to him or to herself. She also let him know that she'd opened her eyes to what he was really made of and appreciated the man he was.

"Mom said I cut you off before you could say much of anything beyond your what-ifs, and when I thought about it, I realized that was true, too," she finished, hoping he'd take up where she left off because she didn't think she could ask him point-blank if he loved her, if he'd had marriage in mind when he'd talked about commitment.

"You said none of my what-ifs mattered," he reminded with an arch to that quirky eyebrow of his.

"I was wrong. They matter a lot."

"Do you love me, Maya?"

He wasn't going to make this easy.

She'd wanted him to declare his love for her first, before she had to. What if she admitted she did love him and he didn't love her in return? What if he kept her dangling the way Shag had done to her mother?

Time to put her money where her mouth was. It was one thing to tell him she thought he was a better man. But this meant she had to trust her belief in his good character enough to be the first one to reveal just how vulnerable she was to him.

Well, she did love him. And she'd come this far. What else could she do?

"Yes, I love you. That's what made it all so terrifying for me. My mother loved Shag Heller. Loved him so much that she let him mistreat her, use her, all while she was still hanging on, hoping he'd eventually marry her. Loving you put me at that same risk."

"Except that I'm not Shag Heller."

"I know. But—" But he still wasn't telling her he loved her.

Shane took a few steps nearer, stopping within arm's reach. "But nothing. I'm not Shag Heller," he repeated firmly.

"I know," she said without qualification.

"And nothing between us is anything like what went on between him and your mother."

"Okay."

Something about that made him smile then, and it was such a relief to see that Maya didn't even care what about her simple okay had caused it.

"I'm in love with you," he said softly, finally.

And hearing the words at last sent a ripple of tingles across her nerve endings.

"I don't want anyone but you," he went on. "Not now or ever. I want you to be my wife. To have my kids. To get old and cranky right along with me."

Relief greater than she'd ever experienced washed over Maya. She closed her eyes as tears welled up in them and threatened to flood for the third time that night. Only these were tears of pure joy. But still she didn't want to cry at that moment.

"Will you marry me?"

"Yes. Yes. Yes," she whispered, her eyes still shut tight.

She felt Shane step closer and pull her into his arms, felt the heat of his big body engulfing her. And with her eyes still blissfully closed, she laid her cheek to his chest, hearing the strong, steady beat of his heart.

"Yes," she said again, making him chuckle.

He tilted her chin up then and captured her mouth with his in a kiss that was very, very soft. But only for a moment. Because in that moment something ignited between them to deepen it, just the way something had ignited between them that first time their hands had touched, and every time they'd come into contact with each other since.

We are combustible, she thought as she slipped her arms around him, under his shirt to the hard satin of his back, and truly gave herself over to him, to his kiss.

It was lucky the coffee table hadn't been replaced because they ended up on the floor again in front of the sofa, just where they'd made love initially. As he explored her body with his hands and his mouth, as she explored him in return, there were different emotions running through her, racing with the passion and desire he was arousing.

It was as if her heart had been unfettered to expand with a new fullness she'd never known was possible. She could feel everything more freely. Give of herself without any hint of inhibitions and revel in all he gave with the knowledge that this was only the beginning of something wonderful, something they would share again and again.

And when he rose above her and joined his body with hers, the pleasure was far greater than it had been before. Richer. Sweeter. More complete as their spirits seemed to soar along with their bodies in unbridled love.

Afterward, as they lay entwined together amid clothes that had been stripped urgently away, Shane groaned deep in his throat, breathing in a long pull of air and sighing it out.

"Tell me you love me again," he ordered.

"You first this time," she teased.

"I love you, Maya Wilson. Body and soul…and body. Forever and ever and ever. Till death do us part. Good enough?"

"Good enough."

"Now you."

"I love you, Shane McDermot. Body and soul… and body. Forever and ever and ever. Till death do us part. And I want the newspapers notified."

"You want it in the headlines?"

"I want the papers and the magazines notified that you are no longer one of the world's most eligible bachelors."

"Done."

"And I want a big wedding."

"The biggest Elk Creek has ever seen."

"So there's never any doubt in anyone's mind that you made an honest woman of me."

"You can lead me around on a leash if you want."

"Hmm. That might be interesting," she joked lasciviously.

He hugged her tighter and kissed her hair.

"I love you, Maya."

She didn't think she'd ever get tired of hearing that. "I love you, too," she whispered, pressing a tiny kiss to his naked chest, knowing without a doubt that this was where she wanted to spend the rest of her life, and grateful that she'd been blessed with a man like Shane to share that life with.

"No more insecurities," he decreed.

As his wife? She couldn't imagine it. "No more insecurities," she agreed.

"And we'll buy your mom a new car as a wedding gift so nobody gets stuck in it again."

"Oh, I don't know. Under different circumstances it might have been kind of nice to be pulled out of it."

"What circumstances would have made it nice?"

"If you hadn't let go of me once you had me out."

He tightened his arms around her even more. "Never again," he promised.

And she believed him. Believed *in* him.

Believed that she was headed for a happy ending to put all other happy endings to shame, because as far as she was concerned, there was no man like Shane. No man who could compare with him.

And he was all hers.

* * * * *

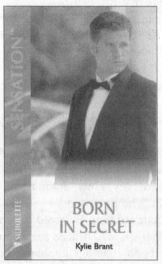

Escape into...
SPECIAL EDITION™

Vivid, satisfying romances, full of family, life and love.

Special Edition are romances between attractive men and women. Family is central to the plot. The novels are warm upbeat dramas grounded in reality with a guaranteed happy ending.

Six new titles are available every month on subscription from the

READER SERVICE™

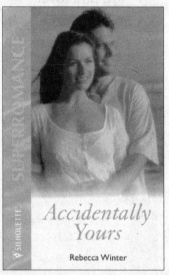

Escape into...
INTRIGUE™

Danger, deception and suspense.

INTRIGUE

SILHOUETTE

SECRET SANCTUARY
Amanda Stevens

Romantic suspense with a well-developed mystery.
The couple always get their happy ending, and the
mystery is resolved, thanks to the central couple.

Four new titles are available every month on
subscription from the

READER SERVICE™

GEN/46/RS1

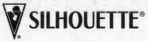